MW01206561

The Moccasin Game

& Other Stories

The Moccasin Game

& Other Stories

Robert Treuer

Loonfeather Press
Bemidji, Minnesota

Cover drawing, "Treuer Shield," by Marlon Davidson
First printing 2000
Printed in the United States of America
ISBN 0-926147-12-9

The Moccasin Game & Other Stories was made possible, in
part, by a grant from Region 2 Arts through funding provided
by the Minnesota State Legislature

Loonfeather Press
P.O. Box 1212
Bemidji, Minnesota

To all Anishinabeg

Migwetch

Contents

THE MOCCASIN GAME

The moccasin telegraph worked well, communication enhanced by chance encounters at the supermarket, the shopping mall, the hardware store, and by telephone. Someone called Howard at his bungalow home on the tribal tract outside the Thompson city limits.

"Whatcha doing, Howard?"

"Looking out the window, watching the corn grow." Howard had a prize vegetable garden each year without weeds. It was the despair of less skilled gardeners because it was just inside the picket fence next to the road where you couldn't miss seeing it. Howard liked to rub it in. He had a contrary streak in his gray and grizzled being. Life was a moccasin game; you had to maneuver through and around obstacles and peoples' mindsets and enjoy the process.

"D'you hear about them digging up these Indian graves where they're adding on to the Emp?"

"Didn't know they were adding on."

"Yeah, big addition. Expanding. Excavators are turning up all kinds of bones, weapons, ornaments. Better come down see." The caller hung up, no name given, but Howard knew it was Stanley from down the road. Callers never said their names on the phone, as though to do so broke a taboo. Saying your own name was impolite, like bragging. This made for conflict in the schools when teachers asked children their names and were met with silence. "Stupid kids don't even know their own names!" they said in the faculty lounge until they had been around a while and knew better, knew that one asked

1

a student to introduce his neighbor. But the custom made phone calls a challenge: do you really know me or do I have to tell you?

Howard shrugged out of his worn, lopsided leather slippers and into tennis shoes, a concession to comfort to which he had been persuaded by the several grandchildren who lived with him and his wife off and on. He ambled the five blocks to the Emporium, headquarters for cheap discount sales, part of a chain.

Once again he mused that the Thompson city fathers couldn't have succeeded better if they had tried to trash the riverbank and lakeshore. The sewage treatment plant, its shrill turquoise settling tanks advertising the nature of the facility, perched atop what should have been a good swimming beach, and the rusty overflow pipe protruded through the riverbank. An asphalt parking lot preempted what could have been a lovely park between the two lakes with the short river connecting them. But no, they couldn't arrange the parking behind the Emp and the supermarket and leave a place of natural beauty to attract the tourists and give pleasure to the year-rounders. Then there was the scrapyard which bought aluminum cans, junked cars, and derelict farm machinery; a crane swung a giant magnet from the never-ending accumulation onto railroad gondolas — right on the banks of the second lake.

"How about you organizing an Indian Day Parade for the tourists?" the chamber of commerce director had asked Howard a few years back. "Feathers, costumes, you know."

"Sure, glad to," Howard had replied to everyone's surprise. Yes, he would line up Indians in regalia, and floats. The works. When the parade posters appeared, the chamber was pleased until someone thought to read the small print outlining the parade route. It wound past every ugly spot in town, missing none—the sewage plant, the scrap yard, the derelict lumber mill, its offal poisoning the water, the junked car assemblage.

"Jesus Christ," the chamber president roared, "that son of a bitching Indian really screwed us!" He dialed Howard who was, as usual, watching his garden grow. "At least you could have taken it past the statue! People come from all over to see that!"

"It's ugly enough, I can add it," Howard offered.

"Never mind," the president grated. "Let's cancel the parade."

"If that's what you want, you got it." Howard was amenable. He hadn't invited any Indians anyhow.

Now he joined the other sidewalk superintendents at the barrier and watched the backhoe dig and scoop in the sand at the edge of the Emp, the gurgle of the river in the background drowned out by the sound of the machine. Most of the gawkers were Indians and Howard elbowed next to Stanley. Even though Howard was only a few inches taller, he seemed twice as wide. Both men wore baseball caps, work shirts, and jeans.

"Thanks for calling," Howard said. "What you got?"

Stanley nodded in the direction of his feet and pursed his mouth. A small heap of stone spearpoints, arrowheads, and remnants of a bearclaw necklace were piled there.

"Didn't touch the bones," Stanley said, "but they're all over the place. Big ones, small ones, skulls. Sickening."

Howard peered into the excavation. "Anybody talk to the manager? The construction boss?"

Stanley shook his head.

"Well, let's." Howard turned toward the store, Stanley at his side, and others trailed along.

The discussion in the manager's office was brief. He phoned the head office.

"In my office now. That's right. No, no question about it. Yes, a lot of Indians. They promised free advertising . . . That's right. Just a minute." The manager turned to Howard. "What do you want us to do?"

"Stop digging up the graves as of right now," Howard, the laid-back gardener most of the time, was gruff. "Call in the state archeologist. Then we'll figure out a proper burial, or reburial."

"You heard?" the manager asked the telephone.

Work on the site stopped but Howard was gone. He returned with a newspaper photographer and was joined soon after by a television camera crew.

"Just some free advertising for you," he told the manager, who scuttled for the sanctuary of his office. "Now I just can't understand why he didn't want to be interviewed. Great big discount chain like that, you'd think they'd welcome publicity. It's good business to advertise."

Two days later the archeologist determined that the bones were from some thirty or more young men, most in their late teens or early twenties. The evidence suggested they had died in a skirmish between Dakota and Ojibwe on the riverbank some 200 years before.

"You can't build a store on top of graves!" Stanley shouted and others agreed.

"Nothing we can do about it," the Thompson Manager shouted back. "It's not city property, the Emporium got a proper building permit. We can't stop them."

The store manager ducked for cover, the Emporium chain spokesman in Chicago said construction would be completed as soon as "appropriate arrangements are made," the tribal council and its chairman Armand Dan tut-tutted the opening of the grave but refused to take an official position since the land was outside the reservation boundaries, and there the impasse stood for ten days. The state archeologist finally negotiated a compromise. All bones and artifacts would be sifted and picked from the dirt excavated earlier, returned into the hole, and many yards of cement would be poured on top, thus permanently sealing the site.

"Lousy deal," Howard muttered, sitting in his armchair and gazing at his garden. "Emporium. Cheap goods at high prices. Imagine walking on graves to waste money on that junk."

No one was at home to hear him. Susie was visiting friends and the grandchildren were in school. He smiled to himself thinking of Susie. They had met at Haskell Indian Boarding School, as had his parents before them. Susie was so petite, so pretty. Even now, more than fifty years later, she was still pretty, though she wore a halo of curly white hair and the slim waist had filled. Her face was young, changed little.

"They wouldn't build on top of the Lutheran cemetery," Howard said aloud, "or the Catholic. But they sure as hell pave over Indian graves." He rocked his armchair harder and harder, then stood up with a jerk that left the chair snapping back and forth.

"Now what trouble are you bringing me?" Armand Dan looked up warily. He had tangled with Howard before and knew from long experience that Howard always made trouble for whoever was in authority. When Armand was an outsider running against the incumbent chairman, Howard supported him, sniped constantly at the incumbent, charged nepotism, which was difficult to refute since everyone on the reservation was related in some way, and accused the incumbent of dipping into the treasury to pay for his boozing and his extended family's debts. Dan loved it and was elected. But he was no sooner sworn in when Howard started needling him. "What trouble you bringing me now?" Dan repeated.

"Why, nothing, Dan, nothing. Just visiting. Such a nice day I had to take a walk, and why not visit my old friend, the chairman." Howard's mellowness was worrisome.

"How come you got such a good garden and nobody ever sees you out there weeding?"

"Just an old Indian trick, Dan." Howard loved the old Indian trick gambit, and his grandchildren asked him who the old Indian was who taught him those tricks. Howard just smiled and shrugged, which was the only answer Armand Dan received. The fact was that Howard always woke early and did his gardening before the sun rose high in the sky, before the bugs came out, and long before Armand Dan and most others went to work.

"I get worried I see you come through that door," Dan said. "It's like you're the Sioux Fifth Column angling t'get us into trouble."

"Got a little economic development idea for you," Howard said, leaning far back in his chair. "The kind of thing you used to campaign about."

"What's that?" Any money proposition interested Armand, and the conflict between distrust of Howard and the possibility of money was mirrored in his face.

This man will never win at the moccasin game, Howard mused, delighted that Armand was twisting on the spit. Howard kept his own expression masked. The moccasin game, ancient Indian gambling sport, consisted of two teams. One hid an object under one of several moccasins, the other team had to guess which one by pointing a stick. Off to the side a singer would pound on a hand drum singing gambling songs as the tension mounted. Large amounts of money or goods changed hands. No, Armand should never play the moccasin game. He didn't have the face for it.

"I see in the papers the State is closing the county landfill. That's a real opportunity for the tribe. Good money." Howard let it hang there.

"I don't get it," Armand said. "You proposing we let them dump their garbage on our land? The State would close that, too."

"You got to think ahead, Armand, think ahead," Howard chided. "They got to ship all their garbage 60 miles to that new incinerator."

"So?"

"So they need a drop-off station, a transfer station. If you offer to build one—and you have a better chance of getting a grant from EDA or some other government agency on account of being an Indian tribe—you'd be doing city of Thompson a favor, you'd be making money by charging drop-off fees; it'd be a good deal."

"I'd catch hell for letting them haul garbage and piling it up on the rez." Armand was thinking, feeling, tasting dollars.

"Who said anything about hauling it to the rez? There's a chunk of land in the city limits over on the east side, just brush. They should let you have it, or lease it for next to nothing, just for the favor you're doing them."

Armand bustled to his file cabinet and returned with a plat book. "Show me."

"Forty acres, right here. No houses, no development. On this gravel road, County 411."

Give Armand Dan credit. Once he sniffed money he'd go after it like a snapper for raw meat. "This makes sense," he said. "I like it. The city'll like it. I'm going to do it. Thanks, Howard, that's a great idea."

"Just be sure when you put it to them, you use the legal description. You know, SW 1/4 of N 1/2, Section whatever, Range 36, Township 142. All that. You talk about County Road 411, or east end of town, people get all upset thinking it's next door to them."

"Good advice, Howard. This is like old times. Thanks."

They shook hands and Howard ambled back home. He had barely settled into his arm chair when the phone rang. Armand had a question.

"What all's involved in building a collection station? Big construction? Big bucks?"

"No, Armand. It's easy. A reinforced concrete slab, and reinforced concrete walls about 10 feet high for, like, bins, about 400 feet square for each bin, open one end for the front end loaders to get in. No roof or anything. Access road or driveway, like circular, make it easy for the hauling trucks to come in. Good job for a couple of guys as attendants."

"That's easy enough. Thanks again." Armand knew just the two men who'd get the jobs, cousins who wanted to move back to the rez from the Cities. And he'd dealt with the concrete people on the housing project and knew he could count on five dollars for every yard the tribe ordered. Howard knew that's what the chairman was thinking and he smiled. Whoever took tribal office fired the predecessor's relatives and hired his own. Armand had done it when he was sworn in, it was expected, but he still had a few relatives wanting in.

Howard smiled again when the Thompson city fathers went for the proposal hook, line, and sinker and endorsed the tribe's application to the Federal Government. On top of it they voted tax increment benefits to the tribe so it would not have to pay taxes on the property until all the loans were paid off, and gave them a 99-year lease on the tract. Thompson really was in a crunch to collect and remove its garbage, and had run out its options and delays on the State's closing the landfill.

The project was funded quickly. It was small, neat, and compact, a timely proposal when costlier ones could not be considered, and it was environmentally oriented. It was clearly for motherhood and against sin, and the government agency could afford it, pointing to itself as a champion of a minority and of environmental integrity at the same time. The district's congressman announced the funding and implied he was responsible.

The collection station was built within five months and Howard went to see it only once during that time, when they poured the ten-inch-thick reinforced concrete slab for the pad.

The city manager was on his way to the grand opening, one arm in his suitcoat sleeve, the other fumbling, when the phone call came.

"Yes," he barked impatiently, halfway into the jacket.

"You the city manager?" the male voice enquired.

"Yes, I am. Who is this? I'm in a hurry."

"Just a citizen. Say, are you really going to pile all that garbage on top or the Poor Farm? There's people buried out there."

"The Poor Farm? What's that? What are you talking about?"

"That place out on 411. It used to be the Poor Farm, where they put the old people, and the ones too sick to work who didn't have relatives. You know, from pioneer days? Early settlers? They had a home there, the Poor House, and this little farm to feed themselves. Died, they were buried there. You check it out. It's true." The caller hung up.

It was true. Tons of hardened, reinforced concrete encapsulated the remains of the early white settlers who had had the misfortune of ending their lives destitute.

"Can't tear it out," Armand Dan said. "Got a contract with the United States Government. You'd have to pay back the money yourselves, we couldn't."

"We what?" the mayor roared. "On top of a cemetery? Didn't anybody check the legal description?"

Someone had, but there was nothing to show it had been the Poor Farm. Legal descriptions only said where a given parcel was located, not the use to which it was put.

"Can we just forget about that Poor Farm and go ahead with the grand opening?" the chamber president said. "Nobody knows about it any more."

"Somebody knew, they called me," the city manager answered.

"The tribal chairman, I bet he knew!" the president said.

"He didn't," the city manager was sure. "Cussed real good when I told him."

Howard, sitting in his arm chair, gazed at his garden, and smiled.

GRAY AND GREEN

I t's hard to be an Indian. Now how many times had he said that in his life? Had it said to him? Sometimes wryly, then mockingly, teasingly, when someone was having a hard time of it wading through deep snow to put a tobacco tie high on a special tree, shoveling a path to the sweat lodge in winter, huddling under a blanket waiting to enter the sweat lodge in the cold with the cleansing wind doing what it was supposed to do but the body unwilling and shivering. Oh, there'd been many times. But always there was the reward for spiritual struggle, always, even when the prayers weren't answered, or answered otherwise than he had hoped, but answered nevertheless because it was in the trying, the reaching out that the connection was made. The granting of requests was the extra fillip of life.

He was tiring, breathing in shorter gasps, using the strength stick with the eagle feather and ribbons tied near the handle as a cane. I won't pause, he mumbled to himself, it's only a few more steps; the lakeshore looks much the same and I'll look at it while I take one step, and another, and give thanks for the water, the source of all life, for all the women who are the caretakers and protectors of the water and who themselves carry future life in the water within their bodies, yes, I will think of that.

But the place was changed. The two big burial mounds had disappeared, shrunk to shallow rises and overgrown with grass and brush. A tattered mattress, its inner springs exposed, partially covered the remains of one. Garbage and litter were strewn about. A little ways away he could see a shack that had not been there the first time, white

9

smoke oozing out the chimney pipe. This is so ugly, so awful, he thought. When we trash creation we trash ourselves, how we think and how we feel; maybe I made a mistake coming after all these years. But no, it couldn't be a mistake, I had the vision to come so it must be right. Indians don't have an imagination, he smiled to himself, they have visions. Oh well, the lake is beautiful, and the sky, and the river still flows by here, and it will feel good to rest. But first he had to put out tobacco. He held the little leather pouch in his right hand, the strength stick pinched between elbow and ribs, and used his left hand for the tobacco.

"Always offer semas with the left," his uncle had taught when he was apprenticing, "it's closer to the heart. And we call it semas, not kinnikinnick." That was before Uncle had taught him to make his own semas from red willow inner bark and the other ingredients.

"Migwetch, Gitchi Manidoo, migwetch Mishomis, migwetch Nokomis," the old man said, presenting his offering to the sky, to the four directions, touching his hand to the earth before sprinkling the contents on what remained of the mounds, thanking the Creator, the grandfathers, the grandmothers. "I come here today, Grandfathers and Grandmothers, to give thanks for this beautiful life, and because I feel called to this place where I had my first fast and my first vision dreams. I come to be with you." Then he cleared a little space in the grass, shoving a styrofoam cup out of the way, pushing three beer cans and a pop can behind a shrub, and sat down.

He saw the girl coming up the path from the shack before she saw him. These Indian girls are so pretty, he thought, but I sure wonder what their lives are like these days. He prodded yet another piece of trash with the tip of his strength stick and watched her approach without looking directly at her, watched her freeze in surprise at seeing him.

"Who're you?" A direct question! She must have been startled.

"Just an old man resting," he smiled. "Come on, sit down. You live down that house." The statement could have been a question, except that there was no other dwelling within miles. "Place looks much the same as when I was here as a boy. Marsh for miles, both sides the river. Except back then the river wound back and forth like a long lazy snake. Engineers must of dug out the channel when they built this dam at the outlet. And ducks, so many you couldn't hear yourself in the spring. Geese, swans, all kinds of birds. And these mounds were big then, real big. That one over there about fifteen feet high, and the other nine or ten. Big."

"What mounds?" She sat down, but not too close.

He pointed with the strength stick, indicating the ancient outlines. "Burial mounds from long ago. Real old. What do they call you?"

"Michelle."

"You got another name too?"

"Awning."

"I meant an Indian name. No? They didn't give one? That's too bad. Maybe you'll get your name some day. Now Awning, let's see, I did know a Tom Awning once."

"That was my grampa," she looked directly at him. "Did you know him? I only heard about him."

"Met once or twice. See, you at least got a part Indian name. His real name was Bright Star, and star, see, the Indian for that is ahnung, that's star. And when the Indian Bureau set up the rolls and gave everybody white names and he said his in Indian, they wrote down Awning instead of Ahnung. So that's how that was. My father, his real name was Bidwaywegeshik and that's like coming clouds, or approaching storm, like the thunder bird is coming. But when he stepped up to the clerk, my dad didn't speak English, so the clerk asked him who he was, and the interpreter says to Dad, he says this man wants to know who you are, and my dad says I'm a young man, that's who I am. In Indian that's oshkinaway, means young man. The clerk thought that was funny and wrote down Skinaway, so that's our name now, I'm Jimmy Skinaway to those people." He waved his stick in the air. "But you call me Grandfather if you want. How come you not in school?"

"Didn't feel like it today."

He saw the beginning of a pout before she bent her head, long black hair masking sad eyes.

"You know your clan?" He wasn't going to allow her to withdraw. "Your dodaim?"

She shook her head. "How'd you get here? I don't see no car."

"Walked. I live down by Three Corners. Neighbor gave me a ride to the boundary road and I walked from there."

"That's a long way! D'you walk just to get to this place?" She said "this place" as though no one would ever go out of their way to the junk pile.

He nodded. "Wanted to see it one more time. Went on my first vision quest over there by that first bunch of trees. Long time ago, I was a boy, about your age, fifteen. Fasted the full four days. These mounds here, you could see them for miles."

"What happened to them?"

"Somebody said the engineers, when they built this road and dam, bulldozed them to use for fill. Bones and all. I didn't come to see that, I just wanted to see the lake and the miles of marsh, with the trees way back along both sides. Here, I'm kind of old and stiff, can you help me untangle these ribbons and tie them up? I'll show you."

They both rose and he handed her a bunch of ribbons of different colors, cut to two-foot lengths.

"Here you put a yellow," he pulled down a willow branch and watched her tie a ribbon to it. "Another knot. Good. Now a red over here. OK. Over there we'll put a blue."

"What are those for?" she asked.

"The four directions. East, now the eagle is east. And the turtle, that's south. That's the interpreter, interprets our words to the spirits, and west, that's the buffalo, guards the way to the spirit world, and the bear's north, he's the healer is the bear."

They sat down and watched the ribbons flutter in the wind. "I rested enough, now let's put up the rest. You put up a dark blue and a light blue together here, good. Now over there you put up a gray and a green. No, not that ribbon, that's almost white, you want a gray, a real gray."

He watched her tying critically. "You sure those knots are good and tight? All right."

"What are those for?" Michelle asked.

"The dodaims, the clans. Each clan has its own colors, just like you get colors for your name. Name colors. You wear them in your clothes, like at ceremonies or powwows, or used to. Then people knew your family, your clan, just by looking."

"I wish I had colors." Michelle watched the dozens of ribbons fluttering all around the area where the mounds had been, from the lakeshore, along the river, and back to the marsh willows.

"Here, you take these two," he fumbled among the remaining handful of cloth strips. "Tie them up in that tree over there," he pointed with his stick. "That's dark blue and white for your name, Ahnung. That shows that you, Ahnung, are showing your respect for the spirit of these people lived here long ago. And they'll know that, and they'll look out for you. Now you come over here. You take these two, the gray and the green and tie them. Good. Your grampa was Mahng Dodaim, that's loon clan. Mahng. That's always been a real strong clan. Leaders, speakers, fighters. Their colors are gray and green, and that's your clan, those are your clan colors."

"How do you know that's my clan?"

"Remembering your grampa."

They sat in silence and when the shadow floated over them the old man did not look up.

"Look, look," Michelle pointed. "It's the eagle, right over our heads!"

"I know, Granddaughter, I could tell without looking." He reached into the tobacco pouch, then made his offering and showed her how to do it. "Migwetch, Migizi," he said, "thank you, Eagle, for honoring us. See, this bird he checks on us, to see if we are doing things in the right way and reports back to the Creator, Gitchi Manidoo. Migizi has to find at least one person each day and report back; if he doesn't find anybody living the right way, Gitchi Manidoo'll let the spirit of darkness destroy this world. At least, that was the old teaching. Well, I got to go now."

"You walking all the way back? Maybe I can get my dad, maybe he can give you a ride." Two "maybes" hyphenated by a shadow flickering behind her eyes.

"Thanks, but those people are going to pick me up by the boundary this evening." He grasped his strength stick and rose.

"That's about seven miles." She looked concerned.

"I know, but it wouldn't be right. I'll go the way I came, walking." So long as he could walk he wouldn't take a ride. What kind of pilgrimage would it be, riding in a car while he could still walk?

"You know, that's a pretty crookedy cane you've got there." She looked at the knobby strength stick. "Only the top of it is straight."

"That stick is like my life, twisted and going this way and that way, until it gets here, to where this eagle feather and the ribbons are. It's straight after that. I fasted many times, entered the sweat lodge many times, before my life straightened out." He gazed at the stick and turned to go, but turned back to her.

"Stand on that leg a minute," he pointed the stick at her left leg.

She stood on one leg but soon began to wobble.

"That's not working so good," he said. "Try the other one."

She shifted to the other leg but soon began to lose her balance.

"You see those two things you call legs?" He pointed the cane at her jeans. "Two of them, right? Hard to stand on just one any length of time. One leg is the teachings, the education you need to live a good life in the real world and help people. The other one is the traditions, the spiritual life inside you, inside us Anishinabe, us Indian people. Need both. Learn the one in school, learn the other if you find some old people, some elders, they'll teach you. Go look for them. You'll find them."

"Like a grandfather," she mumbled to herself and the old man did not hear her.

He turned then and walked out to the road and away. Slowly but steadily, thinking he should have told her more, much more, told her it's hard being Indian but even harder if you're born Indian but don't have the strength of the traditions, the feelings that come from the belonging. But he kept on walking, figuring she'd find that out, figuring she had already had a taste of what it was like being born Indian without being taught the ways. Maybe he'd given her an inkling of the beauty part of it.

She watched him hobble away, ribbons and feather jarring and fluttering with his every step.

"Good-bye, Grandfather," she murmured.

When Michelle came out in the morning to wait for the school bus there was no sign of the old man. The ribbons were still fluttering in the brush, and she could glimpse the many colors waving in the breeze. The sunlight glittered on the lake and the marsh grass undulated in the wind like ocean waves. She was wearing a gray skirt and a green sweater.

MOIRA

Trouble with omens, you never knew until afterwards whether it was one or just some random event, or whether it was meant for someone else. By then it was too late anyhow. When Butch pulled the net a loon was caught in it along with the fish, dead, drowned after struggling to free itself. It had torn the mesh but couldn't get free, wings and one leg trapped in the twisted strands. The net he could mend but no way could he breathe life back into the dead bird.

His heart sank as he held the once beautiful caller and swimmer, and he had the impulse to throw it into the water. Then he thought better. It would have to be put out with tobacco and cloth, strips of green and gray for the Loon Clan.

"Pitiful," Butch muttered. "Too bad, Cousin. Was you hungry? Too anxious for the fish to look out for the net? Too young t'have learned? And my own clan, too. Oh Cousin, oh. In all of this great lake did you have to come to die in my fishing net?"

Alone in the boat—he always fished alone, the strongest man on the reservation—he cradled the dripping bird to his chest as he motored through the lifting morning haze, heading for the little dock jutting out by his house. People would have wondered seeing him hold the bird thus; they took him to be stoic and unmovable, a giant who rarely spoke, a homely man with pockmarked face and stubble-cut hair. It never occurred to anyone that his seeming taciturnity was really shyness. And here he was in the boat clutching a dripping wet bird corpse to his chest and muttering to it lovingly, calling it Cousin and friend and wishing it peace in the spirit world, promising to set out food for the spirit journey.

"Fish, some nice small fish the kind you like," he said but there were tears in his eyes as he said it and foreboding in his heart. It was an augury, the dead bird a sacrifice predicting, prophesying something for someone. It was aruspicy, divination of the future from the dead bird. But what future? Whose?

He heard the zuzurring voices of child and wife above the purr of the idling motor and coasted in. The dock was next to the lower part of the house which he had built into the clifflike shore. No one could figure out how Butch had crafted the house, the best in the village, perched on the rock, perched into it, really, as though it had always grown there, been a part of it all. He had done it all by himself, a labor of love for the woman he had brought home from the Cities one day to everyone's surprise.

This quiet man who hunted and shared the meat, who guided whites eager to bag a moose or catch a trophy fish, who had never married or lived with a woman, had gone shopping for parts and come back with the raven-haired beauty. She wore a leather jacket, tight jeans, and motorcycle boots incongruous on her tiny feet, and she looked Indian.

"But I'm not," she explained when asked. "Maybe some Sioux back there somewhere." It sounded vague, ambiguous, as did all her responses to the subtle and not-so-subtle probing of the other women. And therein lay part of the problem. They did not like her, even though she looked more Indian than some of them and became involved in beadwork and quillwork and was better at it than anyone, more Indian than they. No one loved her for it, but they respected her skill, her hard work, her caring for Butch and·later for the child.

She looked as though she had ridden postilion on motorcycles, and so she rode now in the social life of the village and in the life of the giant who had brought her home and doted on her with a fatuous smile permanently pasted on his hitherto expressionless face. So it was that he wrought the miraculous house out of cliffside and logs he felled, peeled, and hauled home to notch. And as the home moved to completion room by room she furbished it with furniture she made and decorations she crafted but never sold to tourists. And Butch never went out on the wild benders that punctuated his bachelor days, roaring binges ending in mayhem or jail or a dewy ditch.

They had no children and offered no explanation. Some women said she'd had herself fixed long before she met Butch, but it was only mean talk. It became known they had applied for an adoptive child because one of the teachers and a shopkeeper were asked for references by the big city agency.

"Foster parents," the social worker declared when Butch and Moira finally passed muster and came to pick up the boy. "Like probation for a year or so, to see how he works out and how you work out. If everything is OK, it goes up for legal adoption. In court and everything."

They didn't care about all that. The boy was beautiful, he was Indian, and he glommed onto Butch like a leech to meat. The big man held the boy as tightly as the boy held him and the tears of joy came from Butch's soul.

"I built a special room for you," Butch said on the drive home, and the four-year-old smiled and the big man smiled. "But you can come snuggle your mum and me. Ours next to yours." They smiled a lot, the three of them, in such happiness that no one thought it odd, the giant with the petite wife and the small boy.

He was a sweet child. The other children called him Eejay for his initials, Earl James, but first the women of the village and soon others preferred the nickname Mahkunce, bear cub, because he climbed up Butch's legs and torso into the arms as a cub climbs a tree. He was eight now, going on nine.

Butch did what he had to with the loon and went inside to breakfast.

"Good catch?" Moira asked.

"So-so."

About midmorning Hummer, the tribal chairman, stopped in. "Help yourself," Moira nodded at the coffee pot. She was sanding a rung for the new chair, parts of which were strewn over the kitchen floor awaiting assembly.

Hummer did, glanced at Moira's handiwork and nodded approval. "Nice." Then he headed for the sound of Butch's hammering.

Hummer was short and portly with a round face, round cheeks, and perpetually pursed mouth. It was the mouth that had birthed the nickname. "Looks like a hummingbird," an uncle had remarked upon examining the infant, and Hummer it was.

He sat on a pile of peeled logs as Butch worked.

"New room," Hummer said. "Expecting?"

"Want a little girl to go with the boy," Butch replied. "We applied, they told us it'd be a while. No little Indian girls right now. Don't hurt to be ready."

It was understood. Most Indian orphans or detritus from broken relationships were taken in by extended family, and few were available. Butch and Moira had not bothered with the legal adoption of the boy and Social Services had enough to do without more paperwork; since all was well, why bother. Meanwhile they were on the lookout for a girl to fill out the family.

"How about coming with me the Cities tomorrow?" Hummer got around to the point of the visit. "Supposed to pick up VISTA volunteers stay with us a year, teach us about civilization and all."

"VISTA?"

"Like Peace Corps, only here in the States. We're supposed to get one or two. St. Paul. Each rez gets one or two, like help teachers in school, or the tribal council. Don't cost anything."

"Gonna get lonesome driving yourself?"

Hummer's mouth pursed extra. "Likely be a girl or two, and it wouldn't look right me alone. Besides Emma'd raise hell."

Now that was truth. Hummer's wife Emma was jealous as long as the sun rose, and it rose every day.

"Tribe'll pay meals and hotel, won't cost you," Hummer cajoled. "Public duty, Butch, good citizenship and all." It was plain Butch preferred staying home to finish his carpentry. "Besides, you're on the Council."

"When?" Butch grudged.

"Tomorrow."

There were twelve volunteers for the six reservations, but the assigning and assorting defied simple arithmetic, much to the consternation of the VISTA coordinator from Washington, who thought he had suitable pairs arranged. One reservation wanted three, another none, and manila file folders containing lists of each volunteer's skills and biographical data circulated among the reservation delegations who looked over the top of the folders to examine the prospects in the flesh.

"Like a slave auction," Hummer murmured at Butch. "Trouble is all these whites look the same to me. Which ones you fancy?"

Butch shrugged. "I'm just along t'protect you."

They were all young, college age, five men and seven women, ranging in size and shape from short to tall, and as bewildered by the process as the reservation delegates. After much paper shuffling and long silences, the coordinator sent the volunteers to the hotel restaurant and the serious business began.

"Ain't gonna work," one chairman said. "You got us down for these two women, that tall one with the mustache looks like she oughta be a man an' that pudgy eighteen-year-old is just a kid. I'm not gonna be responsible for that pair, I'll take one or t'other, but not the two. That's just askin' for trouble."

The taller of the women was in her mid to late twenties, a tanned, lanky person nearly six feet tall and it was true, there was something masculine about her wide shoulders and bearing. Yet she had appeared animated and open in her conversations with the tribal representatives and the other volunteers, and well-liked by her peers. In contrast the youngster of the group was quiet, almost sullen in her silence, as quiet as Butch but unlike him, watching, watching, watching all going on about her, a secret energy soaking it in, absorbing it, digesting it all in a cabalistic ritual privy only to herself. No taller than Hummer, with blue eyes and a kewpie face framed by light brown curls, she appeared young and vulnerable compared to the worldliness of the mannish older woman.

The coordinator blushed and spluttered. No one wanted to say the word "lesbian" but it hung in the air unspoken.

"We'll take the tall one," someone spoke up. "She got good credentials, teacher certificate and two years at a Pueblo school."

"But that'll give you three," the coordinator said.

They argued and bargained mildly, good-naturedly. It was fun for the representatives—they did not often get to hire anyone. That the coordinator's bureaucratic plans foundered made it all the nicer.

"We'll take the kid," Hummer finally spoke up. "Solo."

They were to leave the next morning. At night in their shared hotel room Butch asked, "Who she going to stay with?"

Hummer looked and pursed his mouth even more. "Forgot. I was going to ask the teacher. Maybe they got extra space."

"She can stay with us until it works out," Butch offered. "Won't be getting our little girl for a while and the room'll be done soon. Sleep on the living room couch until it is. Might be fun for her, with Moira and the kid. Homelike."

Hummer's symbiotic impulse toward the young VISTA volunteer was short-lived, lasting not quite three weeks. Her Ohio corn-fed dimples and short-statured body were vaguely reminiscent of his own build, a distant relative in body shape, but there it ended.

"Nobody can get her to do nothing," he complained to Butch. "Not the teacher, the preacher, the community action director. How's she around your place?"

"All right," Butch was nonplussed. "No trouble."

"She do anything? Help? Play with Mahkunce?"

"No, just sits around mostly, follows Moira around. Moira don't mind her."

The women of the village did not mind her either after the first wary examination. She was clearly no threat where the men were concerned, and if she was lazy then at least no one was out anything.

Her name was Julia Johnson but no one called her by name, there was no occasion to do so. When talking about her she was The VISTA. If she was no help at least she was no bother.

At Butch's she ignored Mahkunce, stayed out of the big man's way, and spent most of her days shadowing Moira or sitting on the couch doing nothing.

The high school coach came by one day. "I really need help," he pleaded with her. "The junior softball team is going to the tournament, Sylvia can't come, her mother's sick, and the assistant coach had to go to Wisconsin."

Julia — it was Julia, not Julie, and she was insistent about it, one of the few topics that drew animation from her—walked back into the house with a heavy tread, not having responded, and returned shortly in different shoes, carrying a jacket and handbag.

"Might as well have left her home," the coach told Hummer the next day. "She just sat on the side pouting, didn't say or do nothing, and got back on the bus when it was over."

"How'd the team do?"

"Won both games, going on to district next week."

"That's good." Hummer smiled and went on his way.

After Butch finished the little girl's room and Julia moved into it he tackled the next project, a boat house large enough for fishing net storage in winter and a work bench. Mahkunce by his side, gofered tools, and the two chattered like magpies. They talked fishing and hunting, animal lore, and Butch told long-dormant stories heard from his father and grandfather.

"Let's go fishing," Butch would say, and they'd take the big boat and fishing rods and work was forgotten the remainder of the day as they headed out onto the lake, rounded the east cape, and trolled Waswaugoning Bay. "Waswaugoning, that means fishing by torch-light," he explained to the boy, who mumbled the word a few times until he could say it.

Butch returned from shopping and called the boy. "Here, see if you're big enough to sight it." He handed the over-and-under .410 shotgun and .22 rifle to him. It was a children's model, small and light, and Mahkunce could stretch to sight it.

"Good enough," Butch said, "you're school age and it's time you learned."

They went for partridge and when Mahkunce made his first kill Butch and Moira had the feast for him. Most of the town came bringing food and presents. It was a joyous time and only Butch relished it more than the boy, who glowed with the glory of it.

"Helping feed the family," Hummer told the boy, and it was high praise. "Becoming a man."

Everyone had something good to say to Mahkunce, a family and a town enveloping its own. Moira gave him a game bag she had made and moccasins of home-tanned moosehide with porcupine quillwork in green and gray.

"Mahng," the boy smiled. "I'm Loon Clan like Dad."

Only Julia was silent, in a corner, taking it all in, being part of nothing as the crowd ebbed and flowed and celebrated.

Months had gone by when Hummer came down with a gallbladder attack just as he was about to leave for an economic development conference. "Butch gotta go for me," he told his family as he was loaded into the ambulance. "It's important, we got a chance at the government grant for the marina and hotel."

Butch didn't want to go, he hated leaving home, hated the long drive, the long meetings, but he went. On the morning of the third day of the conference he was called out of the meeting.

Hummer and the coach awaited him in the hallway. Hummer was hollow-eyed, the coach pale-faced and unshaven. They had driven all night.

"They let me out after a day," Hummer said. "Just n'attack."

The three stood there. It was awkward and in the quiet the blood pounded against eardrums like Lake Superior at the shore.

"Is it the boy?" Butch finally spoke into the silence of it.

The coach shook his head. "I got this letter for you," he said. "Let's go someplace for you to read."

They found an unused lounge and Butch opened the letter. His big fingers palsied as he tore at the flap. He had finished only half when it dropped to the floor and he buried his head in his massive arms and wept.

He wept the six hours of the drive home, Hummer driving Butch's car.

"I love Julia the way I never loved anybody," Moira had written. "We're going to the Cities to live. I'm taking the boy with me."

Butch holed up in the empty house three days. He left in the middle of the fourth night and returned with the boy a day later. It did not last. Social Services came for the child.

"You can't take him, he's my son!" Butch roared, and Mahkunce clung to him, shrieking and screaming. Then they both went for their guns. The social workers fled before the giant and the excruciating agony of father and son, but they returned with the sheriff and five deputies the next day and tore them apart.

Everything failed. Butch tried the courts but they told him the adoption had never taken place legally. "You have no standing," they said. "You were just a foster parent. You have no wife, so now you can't be a foster parent any more."

All the letters from clergy, teachers, and tribal officials failed. The pleas were politely rejected.

Butch stopped fishing. He stopped hunting, stopped talking, and walked around like an automaton. He started drinking, and it was violent and awful, doing mayhem to others and to himself. He tried to find the boy to steal him away, go away with him to anywhere, but they had hidden him too well.

To watch this big man was to see a silent scream of pain louder than any noise.

The coach and preacher teamed up and caught Butch on the rebound from the dry heaves on a morning after. They took him to the coach's for a hot bath, shave, and breakfast, and talked to him, saying all the things they could say. Butch looked at them and said nothing, but finally he nodded, got up and left.

He didn't drink after that, and he kept himself clean and did a bit of work, enough to feed himself. It lasted a few months and then he disappeared, fell off the face of the earth.

The house was clean and closed neatly, unlocked as always. There were no notes, no clues. The boat was there, everything was in place. They looked, the sheriff looked, but he was gone without a trace.

"That tall VISTA they was all worried about," Hummer said to the coach one day, "wasn't nothing outta line with her. She worked good, fell in love with a guy, they got married and she's schoolteaching. Who'da thought . . ."

Who indeed would have thought that an eighteen-year-old anti-social kewpie-faced girl would, could, seduce a mature woman, a leather-jacketed petite postilion rider, partner in a family, member of a community? And take her away with her? And she the one they had worried about, had felt a need to protect?

Seven years later they found Butch, as much as could be found. Two men from the rez had gone on a long moose hunt, and way back in the brush, miles from the village, there it was.

He had cut a popple and peeled it, carving a loon into the top of it, a gravestick, and planted it in the ground. It was weathered gray, but the carving was clear. Next to it was the boy's over-and-under

.410 and .22, barrel stuck in the ground. There were no bones or human remains.

"Animals must have got it all," the sheriff said. They looked long and someone came up with a brass belt buckle. "Guess he killed hisself."

The Indians who were veterans looked at each other and looked away. They didn't want to tell the sheriff he was wrong; it would have been impolite. But a warrior knows that a rifle stuck in the ground barrel-first meant a fallen warrior, like a lance point down. They knew what had happened. The gravestick said it. Butch had gone out to fast, not for a vision—for he had had that—but to the death.

The loon was dead, the aruspicy fulfilled.

RESTITUTION

Chickee was twelve the week after Christmas, small for her age but showing first signs of growing up.

"Ma, my chest hurts."

Bernadette thought it was a cold, but it turned out to be something else. "That's your nipples. You're beginning to become a woman." She looked down at her daughter, ebony hair, eyes so dark you couldn't see the pupils. "Time for your berry fast this spring, my girl."

Once a girl's menstruation began so did her one-year abstinence from wild berries. She would pick, and put by, four varieties for a family-and-friends feast marking the end of the fast and the beginning of womanhood. The berries of course represented fecundity, the abstinence a spiritual and physical preparation for the roles of an adult woman.

"Aw, Ma! I don't wanna!" Chickee pouted.

Sam pretended he hadn't heard. The girl would be embarrassed at the same time she was pleased. He liked it that Bernadette was passing on the old ways. The Indian teaching about menstruation made it a time of special power, the monthly renewal and refurbishing Manidoo's gift to women empowering them to birthe. It was a time for women to stay apart, lest the awesome force given to them weaken the men.

Chickee also knew her monthly you-know-whats would start, that she would join the circle of women around the fire at the time of the full moon, offering woman prayers and burning the cloth offering in the monthly renewal ritual mirroring the sloughing within her womb. And she knew some other things about being female she didn't want to think about and would never ever say aloud.

"Strawberries on that slope south of the wood pile," Sam said from across the room. "Might even show you my own private blackberry patch. You know where there's blueberries, chokecherries, pincherries."

Chickee didn't acknowledge that she heard her dad's attempt at helpfulness and wandered to the TV, turning on cartoons extra loud.

Mixed feelings about growing up, Sam concluded. Bernadette looked serious, almost sad as she continued watching the child, now sullen and within her secret self in front of the screen.

"She's been making a fuss about going to school for a while too," Sam said to Bernadette over coffee at the kitchen table. "She worried about taking the bus to Runner next year?"

"I dunno. She hasn't said." There was a hint of evasiveness in Bernadette.

"Used to love school, couldn't wait to get there," Sam continued. "Now the grades are slipping and you just about have to drag her."

Bernadette nodded and stared into the half-empty coffee cup. When they sat across the table from each other like that, they looked to be the same height, but walking through the village Sam seemed much smaller. Actually the height difference was less than two inches, but he was a thin man, sinewy and tough, and neighbors asked his help with the difficult and heavy work. He had a hawk face in profile, but he was as spare in body as he was with talk. Yet they all came to him for his calm receptivity as much as his skills and strength.

Now with Bernadette it was different. She was just plain big with a full and wide face, and from there down everything was wide. From early childhood on, somewhere in grade school, she'd developed vivid coloring and facial hair. Her eyebrows were so full that other women would have plucked them, but she didn't. Her hairline plunged down her brow in a widow's peak, and she was darker than most others. Even her lips were a purple shade. She and her sister Betty, who was not quite so round but taller, wide-shouldered and long-waisted, periodically fought the good fight to take off a few pounds. A few times they went to Overeaters Anonymous, but the 29-mile drive to the county seat town of Runner was too much of a bother.

"I'm not short," Sam would joke in repartee if anyone made a remark about his height. "It's just my legs are short at one end."

Bernadette would periodically bemoan her weight, vow a draconian regimen, but when you worked as Headstart cook that was easier said than done.

Sam and Bernadette had always stressed schooling, and the two boys had heeded and done well. Peter had won a scholarship into the University and was doing well in math and the sciences, but beginning to talk about going on to law school. Paul was in the service teaching at an electronics school. Chickee had started off well but now, in sixth grade, a change had taken place.

The village school was good. Everyone said so. It had been a Bureau of Indian Affairs institution when the agency was headquartered at Onigaming, which in the Indian language meant carrying place, or portage, in reference to the narrow neck of land near the base of the long, sickle-shaped peninsula jutting into the lake. Carrying a canoe across there saved a lot of paddling time in the old days. Onigaming was at the end of the peninsula, a little over a mile across the deep water from Runner but 29 miles by road. The little children did their grade school at Onigaming, then took the bus to Runner from seventh grade on.

The little school was presided over by Teacher, a diminutive blond, blue-eyed, Scandinavian with owl glasses that did not stop him from leaning forward to peer at everyone and everything, although he never looked you in the eye. He was a very religious man and taught Sunday School at the Baptists, helped by his even more diminutive wife who also assisted at the school. Both of them were religious, and their children knew better than to be different from the parents. Teacher had been there since he finished college (or was it a seminary?), now going on twenty years. He was so good you couldn't fault him. The little children loved him, and everyone knew he loved the children, who sat on his lap and cuddled up to him, the very little children especially. There were people in the village who had to think hard what his real name was because no one ever called him anything but Teacher. In the outside world he was Einar Thorkelsen and his wife, who had been a Swanson, was Elena.

"I've taken to walking her to school," Bernadette said, still entranced by the coffee in her cup, "but it's like pushing a car uphill."

There was something in her not looking at him that made Sam uneasy. It gave him a feeling that too much was unsaid, that something was being held back, but it went against his grain to pry and poke trying to fish out what would not be hooked anyway.

"I'll call Joe to cover for me tomorrow morning and take a turn walking her to school," Sam finally said and got up.

Sam had worked as janitor and maintenance man at the Runner school since his early twenties. He was the only Indian with a job in town for a long time, the community's token against the prejudice everyone knew was there. He was patronized, referred to as a "good Indian," and his quiet ways gave the illusion of his consent to the stereotyping. On the outside Sam was polite, sometimes joking in his dealings with them. In his heart he shunned them as they shunned him.

Bernadette, Betty, and some of the other women found strength to cope within a predominantly white world through the spirituality and traditions of the old ways. They obtained teachings from elders such as Aunt Emma, some two- hundred miles north in Canada. They entered the sweat lodge regularly, went on fasts, made their cloth offerings over the full moon fire each month. Sam and the other men approved, but did not practice.

"You and Rory ought to get a men's circle going," Betty would taunt Sam. "Do you good. Shouldn't just be us women keeping Indian ways." Shy Bernadette would watch Sam closely for a sign that he would finally do something about it, but it was usually left to her aggressive sister Betty to prod, for all the good it would do. "Take out your pipes, sit around a fire and pray."

Sam would nod, smile, and do nothing, partly from inertia, partly because of ingrained reluctance to be assertive and take the lead. He would have entered the sweat lodge, fasted, done some of the things he had seen his father, uncles, and grandfathers do, put down his tobacco and pray, but he waited for some other man to start something. Meanwhile the ancient pipe given by his dying father remained wrapped in flannel while Benadette and Betty brought out theirs whenever the women gathered, which was often. "Right," Sam said once again. "We really should." Not would, but should.

When he walked Chickee to school next day a misty fog hung over the lake lending an air of mystery to the landscape, little of which stood out as discernible shapes. What could be out there beyond the next few feet? What could be inside the human heart? Sam took his daughter's hand in his own and found hers limp and cold. But soon it warmed and returned the clasp.

He could feel her slowing down as they came closer to the white clapboard building, slowing more as they passed the big bell set in a trestle on the playground, a bell that also served as community tocsin and fire alarm. As they came to the steps Chickee tore her hand away, turned her back to Sam, and bent over to retch. He tried to comfort her through the dry heaves but she wouldn't have it.

"I'll take you home," Sam said.

She shook her head. "I'll be all right, Da. Really. I'll go, I want to." She left him to enter the school.

Sam looked at the empty doorway, bereft of understanding, longing to enfold and comfort his child. Other children drifted through the haze and around him, so wrapped in their own words and worlds they scarcely noticed him, almost like the whites in Runner.

Sam had the door of his car open when he heard Rory's truck polluting the air as it approached.

"Trouble getting up before breakfast?" His brother-in-law stuck out his head. "Never known ya to be late or miss a day."

Sam shook his head no. "Walked Chickee t'school for once. You know your radiator's steaming? Boil over at that rate."

"I'll wait until it does." Rory was huge, so big it was a wonder he fit into the cab. He climbed out now to chat, not even bothering to look at the rising steam. Rory's rebellion against society, and it was a self-defeating one, was never to fix anything until it was absolutely necessary, if not too late. His nickname had come in his early teens when any vehicle he drove lost its muffler in the woods. Silent approach and Rory's cars were mutually exclusive.

"New thermostat would fix that. I could help you," Sam said, knowing immediately it was a futile offer. They chatted amiably a few minutes and went their ways, Rory to cut pulp and Sam to Runner.

Chickee ate her usual supper that night, small portions, some of which remained behind, and then baffled any connection with her parents, as she now did, by tunneling into a television program. Just before bedtime she hauled her schoolwork to the kitchen table and scribbled away at it, but it looked to be something done in sufferance in a slapdash way.

The parents sat over their late night cup of coffee and Bernadette looked askance at Sam. She could tell he had something on his mind.

"Walked her to school and at the door she got sick," he said. "Threw up."

Bernadette had been looking at him, but now her eyes shifted, flicking from side to side as if checking for a reaction, for a further sign, but then avoiding eye contact as though to hide her thoughts. Sam could tell. He could always tell when she was keeping something secret. It made him sad and uncomfortable on the rare occasions when it happened, because it was a strange phenomenon to him who expressed himself by words, or body language, or behavior, and had no such needs. What he could not see was the trembling of Bernadette's hands under the table.

Bernadette was unable to find alone time with her sister Betty until both finished work the next day. Betty worked half days, usually mornings, as a homemaker calling on the elderly at their homes. She checked their medications, cleaned house, cooked an occasional meal, but mainly visited. Many of her clients were lonely and lived in isolation, remembering days long gone.

"That Chickee's looking more like you every day," Betty said. "Be a beautiful girl." They sat in Betty's living room, having the house to themselves. "Spit it out, Bern. You look like there's a thundercloud over your head."

"Don't know if I can. I got to but I can't make myself say the words."

Bernadette's weeping started as a seeping, tears trickling down her round cheeks, and then she couldn't stop. It was sobs and heaving, wracking exhalations and intakes of air. Such anguish, such pain shook her chest she could control them no more than she could stop the wind. Betty crossed to sit closely beside her on the couch, but she did not touch her sister, allowing her instead to exorcise and express whatever it was that was there.

"You were two years ahead in school," Bernadette finally croaked, her throat raw, and she blew her nose on a tissue Betty handed her. "Oh God, I hate this. Did Teacher ever, like, you know, do anything wrong with you?"

"Why d'you ask?" Betty sat rigidly, carved out of stone and icy cold.

"He did me. And . . . and . . . now I think he's doing it to Chickee." Bernadette tried to say it out loud, plain, but it was so hard that she screamed it. The words echoed from the ceiling, bounced around the room, flew from the floor back to the ceiling, up above them to that mythical place where the creator who made this earth and all on it, including us, resided.

"Oh shit!" Betty spat. "The son of a bitch. Yeah, he did me. I thought I was the only one, I never even guessed. So you, too. Maybe others. You better tell why you think he's doing Chickee."

They talked then, the sisters, and compared their experiences. Bernadette wept and Betty cursed. They speculated who among their friends might also have been victimized by Teacher and, now that the secret was out, wasted no time in going from house to house among their friends and former schoolmates who still lived in the village of Onigaming. They found five, and two of them had daughters in the little school.

"Hi Auntie," Chickee opened the door that night and smiled, for Betty was her favorite relative and more. She was teacher of the old ways, confidante, elder, and friend. "Bendigeen, come in," Chickee said in Ojibwe.

"You look nice," Betty smiled and put her arm around the girl's shoulder.

"Ma's in the other room doing quillwork," Chickee explained. "I'll get her."

"I'll see her in a while. Let's you and me visit first, I haven't seen you t'talk to in a while." They settled on the couch.

Betty wasn't built to be roundabout and got right to it. "Long time ago I was little going to school here," she plunged in. "Not really big for my age, that came later. We had this teacher was so kind and loving made me feel I was something special. Giving treats, sitting on his lap. Oh he was so nice. I just loved going to that school. He'd say how he liked me, really loved me he'd say. That went on a long time. Then one day he said if I loved him the way he loved me, I would do something special for him. Just to show I really meant it."

Chickee, big-eyed but with her mouth clamped shut, began fidgeting but Betty continued.

"He made me do something to him was just awful. I felt like dirt. I walked out of that school feeling sick but I couldn't tell anybody, they wouldn't believe me. Everybody was always saying what a good teacher he was, and church too, real religious and teaching Sunday School. I didn't want to go back to that school any more."

"Is that why you dropped out?" Chickee asked.

"That's it."

"Was that teacher the same as Teacher?"

"One and the same, my girl."

"Oh." Chickee mulled it over. She ground her teeth and clacked them together. "Auntie, what was it he made you do?"

"Before I knew it he had my head in his lap and both his hands on my head, bending it down. He had his fly open and his thing out and made me put it in my mouth. He made my head go up and down and then this sticky stuff came in my mouth, and he quit. Said it was just something special between him and me, to show I loved him, and not to tell anybody."

Chickee turned her face away. Betty could tell the child was gagging from the heaving shoulders and throttling sounds.

"You can tell me, Chickee," her auntie said. "It would have been better for me if I had told. Saved me a lifetime of grief. Is that what he did to you?"

"Yes," she whispered. "I'm sorry. I'm so sorry. It's all my fault."

"It's not your fault. You weren't responsible for it. He was. It's his fault." Betty's eyes were blazing. "He's been doing it all the years he's been here and it's going to stop. Right now."

"Don't tell Ma and Da, please!"

"Oh, your ma knows. At least, she suspicions. She came to see me today and we talked. That's how it came out. I'd never told her what he did to me. He did it to her too."

Chickee was incredulous. "My ma?"

Betty nodded. "This man is sick. He's bad. He's hurt a lot of girls."

"I don't know. I don't want to get him in trouble. I don't want people to know." The child looked confused, her dark cheeks flushed, and she bit her lip.

"Hey, Bern, come in here," Betty called out, and when Bernadette came into the room Betty gave a slight nod.

The two women flanked the girl and embraced her, enveloping her. "We won't let him hurt you ever again," Bernadette promised her daughter.

"Or anybody else!" Betty vowed.

They told her it would be hard and it was, but they were with her, closely, every moment.

"It's a waste of time," the doctor at the Indian hospital on the other side of Runner said. He was miffed at being rousted from an evening at home and his breath smelled of alcohol. "There's no physical evidence after oral rape. Why put the kid through an exam. Hasn't she had enough?"

"Because the law says there has to be an exam," Betty snapped.

When the smear swabs had been taken and the doctor told them they could go home, Betty said, "One more thing. Here are the clothes she wore. You take a sample off her blouse. She spit the stuff out and got it on her clothes."

"It won't do any good," the doctor grudged.

"Do it anyhow."

No one had been prosecuted for raping an Indian in Runner in anyone's memory, and the part-time prosecutor was not inclined to start now. But two things were against him: the strict new state laws dealing with the sexual abuse of children, and the grim women and three children confronting him in his office. And behind the women there might well come the men.

He need not have worried. Teacher collapsed like a wet rag and confessed to more than anybody would have guessed, told more than Runner wanted to hear, and the trial was pro forma, a plea of *nolo contendere*. It was all handled very quietly, very fast. The superintendent of schools for the Runner district spoke highly of Teacher, expressed sad, hangdog regret over "these unfortunate charges" and said Teacher would always have a job with the district. The minister spoke warmly of Teacher's many good works with barely a nod in the direction of the charges, as though they were the unpleasant besmirching of an innocent by malevolent persons beyond the pale of acknowledgment.

The judge imposed the mandatory sentence and stayed it on condition of treatment and probation. Teacher disappeared. He was gone, no one knew where, and if his mousy wife had knowledge she did not share it.

The great cleansing cold enwrapped the land, snow cushioning the resting earth and the sleeping seeds it contained. Keewaydin, the north wind, massaged the trees. At night the thick lake ice boomed and people in their prayers addressed the great bear who lived in the north, asking him to bring healing to all creation, people included, for Makwah, the great bear, brought healing for the people as did winter for the earth.

A day came when the base of tree trunks wore rings of brown as sun warmed the bark and the encircling snow shrank back. It was like a marriage ring announcing the wedding of trees and earth, reconfirming the relationship, holding a promise of spring and new growth.

Chickee must have grown three inches and was nearly as tall as her mother. She had continued to fill out too. But she had become quieter, more withdrawn into herself despite all efforts by Bernadette and Betty to get her to warm up. The girl went through the motions of obedience and responsiveness but there was no heart in it. The two women would look at each other and their shoulders sagged in defeat; it seemed a replay of their own lives when they had hoped for better for Chickee, and they did not know what to do.

"She just ices me," Betty said. Inside the girl it was perpetual winter, as in the garden of the Selfish Giant.

It was even harder for Sam. Accustomed to Chickee's earlier cuddling, affection, and open love, he was now kept distant. He bore the hurt in silence and it inflamed the silent rage he bore Teacher, that trusted steward of his child who had violated both the trust and the child.

Even Rory, least sensitive of persons, remarked that the joy of life seemed to have gone out of Chickee. "No bounce," he said.

"I wish Auntie Emma was here, she'd know what to do," Bernadette said one day.

"Right," Betty replied. "We'll do it."

"Do what?"

"Ask her to come. Let's drive there and give her tobacco."

It took more like five hours to make the usual four-hour drive to Canada. There were icy patches on the road and pure glare ice on the last seven miles of backroad shaded by trees leading to the old woman's house. They made the trip on a Saturday when neither had to work, thinking they's return that night.

Aunt Emma, tiny round butterball with long gray hair, bright brown eyes, and chubby pink cherub's cheeks smiled welcome from her doorway. She did not seem surprised to see the two women, just pleased. People from all over were always coming to Aunt Emma for advice, for teachings, for sweats, to be put out to fast a mile or so back in the woods. Aunt Emma's welcome mat was always there in the ancient Indian way. She shared food, shelter, her knowledge and wisdom, and her love, no questions asked.

They had coffee sitting at the kitchen table and reminisced. They talked and giggled about the first time they had come to Emma's to have her put them out fasting, and Emma's gentle scolding for sitting together and chatting instead of staying in their individual little bough lodges to meditate. They remembered times when Emma had done teachings, instructing the women about berry fasts and full moon ceremonies, about how the sweat lodge had been given to the people, why Migizi, the eagle, flew over the world in the early light before daybreak. They fell silent and sipped coffee in the quiet.

"We brought tobacco," Betty put a full red pack of pipe tobacco in the middle of the table. It would have been presumptuous to have handed it to Emma. You had to offer it, say what you wanted, and then the elder could pick it up or leave it, signifying whether the request would be granted or not.

"There's this man hurt Chickee," Bernadette began.

"Hurt others too," Betty interrupted, "us too, when we were kids." The anger rose in Betty's voice.

Auntie sat, hands folded in her lap, listening to it all. She searched their faces from time to time, but mostly she looked at her hands, work and age-gnarled, finger joints beginning to be arthritic.

The telling done and the quiet long, Auntie said, "Joe's been sick. He has to go to Winnipeg Sunday afternoon for an operation Monday."

She couldn't come back with them, then. The tobacco still lay in the center of the table, a mountain of disappointment to the two supplicants.

"You can sleep here tonight if you don't have to be back right away," Auntie said in her soft, rich voice.

Betty and Bernadette nodded, and Auntie reached for the tobacco.

They had a Healing Sweat in the lodge behind Auntie's house. Her nephew had been called over from his house down the road to be fireman, and Auntie's sister Sarah came over to be the fourth; you had to have at least that many if you could.

"This is going to be different," Auntie said after the tarp had been lowered over the sweat lodge doorway and the first hot steam was rising, the first few cups of water having been poured to quench the thirst of the grandfather rocks, red hot from the wood fire. "It'll be hard."

She sang the invitation song, asking the spirits not to be shy and to come in with them, the second verse urging those in the lodge not to be shy either. Then she sang of the birds. "Don't be sad, the birds love you." It was a simple verse but significant, speaking to the loneliness, the aloneness of those who had been hurt, reassuring them they were loved. Auntie sang the Indian words softly but her voice carried, borne by the resonance of the Little Boy water drum she pounded in the heart-beat rhythm.

"Ni kanagana," she said at the end. "All my family."

"Ni kanagana," the other three replied, acknowledging the lessons learned.

More water took the redness out of the grandfathers. The steam became thicker, hotter, and the sweat streaked from every pore. It became painful to breathe, it was so hot, but not too hot. Sometimes it took pain to cleanse the body and the spirit.

"I know about abuse," Auntie said. "I had to learn to talk about it, about the things that happened to me, about the things I did. This had to be done so I could learn to leave them behind me, so I could shake free. We are supposed to come into this sacred lodge leaving our bad feelings behind, feelings we don't always know we have."

She prayed then, in Indian, for the spirits' help in the healing and sang two more songs.

"Now we'll go around. I'll pass the eagle feather and when it comes to you, you pray. And then you talk about what happened to you, and you can cry, or scream, the spirits always understand."

What happened to them? They had come for help for Chickee and the other girls!

"Go ahead," Auntie said. "You offer it and the spirits'll take it, send it far away into the sky so it can never hurt anyone else, ever again."

Betty was first, but she sat mute. Outspoken, aggressive Betty could not find words. For this tough and powerful woman brimming with anger and rage it was too hard to let the pain feelings out. They had been held in too long.

Finally the silence was unendurable and Betty spoke into the steam, the heat rising from the grandfathers. "Teacher hurt my little niece Chickee and she's . . . she's . . . "

"This is about you," Auntie said. "Your pain. I'll be praying for the girl after a while. You're in a healing sweat for you. You can't walk the road of life, your feet caught in a rabbit snare of bad feelings, it's against the teachings. People leave those things behind when they come in this lodge. But this healing sweat is different, the spirits'll help you get rid of the snare. Now you go back in time. You think of the bad things happened, say them, relive them, and the spirits'll help you shake free."

It took some doing, but when Betty finally cut loose her screams startled the firekeeper outside the lodge. They were so intense, so piercing, that he fought the impulse to run from them but instead leaned against the outside of the lodge, his palms flat against the sides, to give his support to the ones inside. Had there been others outside, they too would have done this to help the ones inside who were suffering.

When it came Bernadette's turn she didn't fight it at all. She got inside her own anger, and then the pain, right away.

The sweat lasted a long time. Auntie Emma kept the steam going with cup after cup of water until they felt they would be scalded, but it never became quite that hot. She took them through the pain and anguish, the misplaced shame, the long-kept secrets; and then she sang the shaking song when they shook their hands, arms, their heads, torsos, legs, until the shaking-free came from way inside. After that Auntie sang the bird-loves-you song again and had them sing along with her, so they would know they were loved and accepted. She had them sing of the butterfly which was the symbol of childhood and innocence, and of joy, so they could taste that which had been taken from them and to which they were entitled.

When they emerged from the sweat lodge they collapsed on the ground, weak and spent, and lay there on blankets, oblivious to the cold.

"You have to be strong yourself if you want those children to become strong," Auntie told them later when they were back in the house. "You want to help them be healthy, you have to be healthy. That's the teaching, that's why you went through this. The spirits came and took all that old stuff away. If you ever go back to it it'll be because you want to, not because you have to."

"What about Chickee? The others?" they wanted to know.

"You'll be different when you get back home, it'll show itself, the difference, it'll help them. Take them into the full moon circle. Help them pray about such things, show them by praying your own prayers out loud and they'll learn that way. Take them into your sweat lodge, regular sweats. I'll come and do a children's healing when I can, when Joe's out of the hospital. I took your tobacco and I'll be there."

That's what they did through spring and summer, and bit by little bit it seemed to help Chickee and the other girls. Auntie couldn't come those months because Joe's operation turned out to be more serious than expected, his convalescence longer, and she nursed him at home.

The girls became freer, less closed when they were with the women, but Chickee was still closed with Dad and it fueled his helpless pain.

They were sitting in the grass next to the sweat lodge, the women and the girls, on a late summer night. It was a clear night with sparkling stars and just a hint of autumn in the smell of the air. It had been a good sweat, the regular kind they did once a week, and they were all chatting and laughing, giggling at somebody's search for glasses which were right on her face. An unfamiliar car drove up and they fell silent, wondering who it was.

Teacher got out. He was alone. He walked up to the women and stood there, looking almost the same as he had a year ago. The women and girls froze.

"Please, please listen to me," Teacher said. "Don't go away! Not yet! I wouldn't blame you if you did, but let me try to make amends for what I've done. Done to you."

Teacher began to cry. They could tell that he tried to stop but he couldn't. They felt awkward watching him as his tears finally subsided and he sat on the ground some distance from them.

"I'm scared to do this, but I have to," he said. They could tell it was true just from the look in his eyes, from his face, and they all relaxed just a little. "I can't undo what I've done. It'll be with me the rest of my life. I wish I could take it away with me when I leave, the harm I've done you. I can't even ask you to forgive me—it happened, I harmed you. Maybe some of you can. Forgive me. Some. At some time. But I'm not asking it."

He started crying again and Betty waited until that stopped before she said, "So what is it you want?"

"To let you know I accept responsibility for what happened, even if I can't make up for it. Let you know, especially the young ones, it's not your fault, not your shame. It's not your guilt. It belongs to me. I've asked God to help me carry this burden, to take it away from you as much as I can. As much as it's given to me to do."

Nobody knew what to say. Just as teacher shifted on the ground, readying to get up, Betty asked what they were all thinking. "Why d'you do it?"

"When it happened, I couldn't help it. I couldn't help myself. I hated myself, I prayed not to, and then I did it again. I prayed I'd be caught, that I'd die. I thought of killing myself many times. When I was caught I was glad. Then in the treatment center, memories came back. I had no recollection all my life. It's an ugly story, I won't tell you the details, but it involves what my dad and my mom did to me, when I was little, from when I was two years old on. Like what I did to you. Other bad things too, different. I don't want to talk about it."

They shifted around in discomfort, not knowing what to say, what to feel.

Finally Teacher said, "It doesn't excuse what I did." Then he stood up and walked away, got in his car and drove off.

Sam walked out of the house when Rory's truck thundered into the yard. It was late for a visit.

"He's back," Rory shouted through the opening where glass should have been. Evil white smoke and fumes clung to the grass, unhampered by any muffler or exhaust system. The radiator was already venting puffs of steam. Sam looked puzzled.

"Teacher. He's back. Talking to the women at the sweat." Then Sam noticed four men sitting in the back of the truck. He got into the cab next to Rory without saying a word.

They caught up with Teacher a few miles down the road and forced his car to the shoulder. Teacher got out, looked at them, looked closely at their faces, and he knew. He nodded.

They took off his clothes and bade him lie on his back in the middle of the road. Teacher said nothing and did as he was told. The truck was started and driven to the middle of the road aiming to straddle him.

"Give me the grippers," someone said, and was handed the shiny lock-pliers from Rory's toolbox. The man crawled under the front of the truck and began to loosen the radiator drain plug until steam hissed out. Someone else was behind the wheel.

Teacher, lying naked in the middle of the road, the truck looming at his feet, said, "Forgive me, Father, I knew not what I did. Forgive them, Father, they know not what they do."

Teacher clasped his hands on his chest in prayer, the drain plug was removed, and the truck moved forward. When the screams began they lasted only a little while, not quite drowned out by the vehicle's noise.

He was found there, on the road between Runner and Onigaming, in the early morning light by a delivery van driver. He had third degree burns from his head to his genitals, which had been virtually boiled away by the searing radiator fluid, and he died in the ambulance on the way to the hospital.

The men's pipes had remained wrapped too long.

GOING WEST

A rchie hadn't been mide', a member of the old religious society, so his funeral wouldn't follow all the rituals, but it would be traditional. This was the unspoken consensus honoring Old Peter, the dead man's father, who was a mide'. The wake would last four days, there would be the old songs and chants, and some friends or relatives would be sitting with Archie during this time, keeping him company before his spirit went west.

The older ones knew and respected Old Peter, and they had known Archie from boyhood. The younger people had never known Archie because he had gone away, disappeared into the maws of the Cities quite a few years ago after his wife died in the traffic accident when Archie had been drinking and wrecked the car. But now he had come home again.

Old Peter was a heavy man for his years and his frame, and it showed when he stood and cane-tapped his way to the front of the hall. Everyone could see the heaviness in his spirit as well, and his grandson David felt a twitch to accompany him but knew this wouldn't be right, so he stayed back while the old man went to inspect the casket and to do what had to be done.

The undertaker had set the shiny oak box on black-draped sawhorses. Old Peter turned and nodded, and some of the Indian men sitting on benches and folding chairs stepped forward and turned the casket to face west. Archie first had to face east, the direction from which the sun rose, the source of life. But now the four days were over and Archie's spirit could begin its journey west after being thanked, being told he was free to go. It was then the difficult westward journey

41

began in the direction of the buffalo spirit to join those who had gone before.

They had not wanted a casket or an undertaker in the first place, but there had been so much fuss from the authorities the last time there was a traditional burial that they decided to appease the powers that be. When the time came to actually bury Archie the body would be taken out of the casket, wrapped in a heavy star quilt, and lowered into the earth to be allowed to return to nature. The casket would be taken to the junk pile and burned.

The lid was open and Archie's face was covered with beaded black velvet. The body was clothed in a blue work shirt open at the collar, and a beaded leather vest. A beaded medallion in floral pattern of green, gray, dark blue, orange, and black against a white background was strung on a leather thong around his neck. A large eagle feather, the stem wrapped in gray and green beading, had been slipped into the dead man's cold hands.

People had filed into the hall all morning, joining the few who had been keeping wake the past three days and nights, sleeping on bedrolls on the floor. Most new arrivals brought food for the burial feast, and while the women wore dresses or skirts, the men were mostly in jeans, workshirts, and workboots.

Silas Johnson and his burly sons had come early. Square-faced and stern, Silas had carried the bass drum himself, nodding at Peter and David in passing and setting up in a front corner. The singers murmured among themselves, the youngest son tapping the rim of the drum with the padded end of his drumstick. No one could hear the muted beat until the other drummers joined. The first song would be drummed, sung softly, but the muffled rhythm was a steady heartbeat, footsteps walking inexorably west.

Fluttering rivulets of conversation ebbed into silence. Even very little children were quiet now.

They sang the Soldier Song, beginning in a high, nasal falsetto, the voices gradually dropping lower and lower through the registers to a deep bass at the end, punctuated by a sharp drum beat. Then, the rhythm unbroken, they sang the tail of the Soldier Song, the reprise of the song's brave heart, and stopped.

Peter stood next to the casket and it was as though he and the body in it were one, bonded and cemented in spirit.

"I want to thank you all for being here." The old man's voice was strangely remote but resonant, the lips hardly seeming to move at all. "I want to say what's in my heart in Indian, but a lot of people don't talk Indian any more, like older people didn't teach it to their kids, it being so hard to be Indian they didn't want their kids to have to deal with that. You see, this boy here we are burying today, he had some brothers and sisters, but they all died when they were babies. We didn't have no doctors or medicines then, just home remedies, and the old Indian medicines, well, we didn't have any new ones to heal the new white sicknesses.

"But this here Archie, he pulled through. He was a scrawny kid, kind of little and skinny, but he made it. Times were bad then with the big timber all over and done, and the Depression, and the land chopped up and allotted and most of it stolen. His mom got sickly then and we had a hard time. No money for food, for nothing. So his mom and I, we thought maybe we should do what they were telling us from the Indian Bureau, send him off to boarding school. Least he'd get three squares a day and there'd be a doctor if he did get sick.

"She didn't want him to go and I didn't either. And he sure didn't. But one day this Indian agent, he come by the house and he says you're not taking good care of this boy, he should be in boarding school and learn something so's he can get along in the white world. So he took this Archie away. And that boy he cried. We could hear him a long ways. And we said at least he'd get food there and be warm.

"So one day and he's only nine years old then he shows up. Don't ask me how he got all the way from Tomah in Wisconsin back home. We were so glad to see this boy we just couldn't let go of him and he said they beat him and locked him in a closet on account of he talked Indian there. And they wouldn't let him come home to visit or nothing. That's why he run away. He must of walked a lot of the way. I don't know.

"But the Indian agent he come back and he says: this boy run away from that good school and he's got to go back, so he took Archie away again and he didn't want to go."

Peter stumped back and forth, gesticulating with one arm, then the other, moving the cane from hand to hand. It was the old oratorical style and he was thinking it all in Indian and then translating to spoken English.

"Well, time went by and we didn't feel right, this boy being so far away and all. So one day I borrowed this Ford coupe with a rumble seat and three of us drove up there and we waited until they had these kids working in the fields. See, they had to do farm chores and raise their own food there. It didn't cost the government much to run those schools, but they still took the money from selling the allotments and said it was to pay for those schools. I seen Archie and hollered to him to run and he did and we took off. He was riding in that rumble seat bouncing around like a butterfly. I stopped after a while and picked up this rock by the side of the road and put it back there with him and I says Archie, you hold on to this rock and listen to it, it's got a lot to tell you from way back when the Great Spirit made this place. And if you want to talk or say anything, you tell that rock. That rock will remember it forever, always, it'll never forget. And that's what that boy did back there in that rumble seat, he talked to that rock in Indian. After a while we stopped again and picked up this big snapping turtle crossing the road and put it in the back too. That's good meat, a big snapper like that, real good. So the boy he had to watch where he put his feet, kind of.

"It was still hard times so when the CCC's come along Archie here lied about his age and they took him in. That was a good place. Good food and all that. Clothes, uniform. He was in that camp over by Rabidoux Lake and those of you still go in the sugar bush in the spring that way, you know the pine plantations just before you get there. He planted that. That's a nice place now. It was burned over back then.

"He grew to be a man there and then he come home. Sowing wild oats you might say. But we ate good. Lots of venison then, and partridge and rabbit. He went in the Army and done fighting in Africa and Italy and France and he got wounded pretty bad right there at the end. He won these here medals I been keeping for him and they belong to him."

Peter turned to the coffin, reached first into the pocket of his shiny old suitcoat to extract the medals— two bronze stars, one silver, and a number of others—and put them in the casket, laying them over the left breast pocket, fussing with them until each was straight and perfectly aligned.

"He come home and married that school teacher and they had this boy here, David, my grandson. When his wife died in that car accident Archie felt so bad he never got over it. Blamed himself for driving that car in the shape he was in. He left that boy here with us and he went away. Went way up to the Cities and went away in his spirit too and never come back. Until now. Even left his jeebig bag when he went. Forgot it or something, because he had it on him every day of his life since he went and fasted as a boy, in the Army and everywhere, until then, and I been keeping it for him, and here it is, boy. It's yours. When you meet the great buffalo guards the west, guards the way to the spirit world, you better have your jeebig bag and say it real strong. Loud. Say your clan, your dodaim, too, so's they can come be with you, give you strength over there. Say Mahng. Say it four times. Loud. Loon. That's us."

Peter places the medicine bundle in its small leather sack in the casket and motions that he is done.

Simon Johnson pulls a metal folding chair up to the casket, pulls it closer, and sits down, leaning toward Archie. Simon talks to him softly in Indian, like friends having an intimate chat. The people can not hear what is said, it is so whispery, but the older ones know. Simon is thanking Archie for all he has done, for feeding his parents and sharing the food with old people in the village, for planting the trees, for fighting for his country. He is telling Archie his work in this world is done and he need not worry or fret, his spirit is free to go now, to go west, and need not linger and haunt the doorways of the living. When Simon is done, and it takes a good ten, fifteen minutes, he takes his chair back to the drum. He turns to the mourners and says, "If you want to come up here and say what is in your heart, now is the time, but don't drop your tears inside the casket or on it." It would not do to have the spirit feel it was not free to go, that the grief of the left-behind ones said they needed him to stay.

They file past the bier and take their time about it. Then the food is brought and all feast with Archie, giving him a good-bye meal to last him through the long journey ahead

"Time to take the feather," Old Peter finally whispers to his grandson.

"Take it . . . out of his hands?" David is nervous.

"Eagle flies the skies. No part of the eagle belongs under the ground. After we're done go out in the woods, hang it up high in a tree. Tie it real good. Tie it so the clan colors show.

He remembers something and turns back to the mourners. "We're Loon Dodaim, so anybody here is that same clan follow me out so we're together. Rest of you can follow behind. And David, you come ahead with me bring the post."

Simon's sons had put down tobacco the night before and cut a popple about four inches in diameter. They had trimmed and peeled it, cutting out a post seven feet long. Near the top they had carved the outline of a loon, and painted two bands around it, gray and green.

When the mourners have left the hall Simon and his sons close the door and spread the star quilt on the floor. They lift the casket down and transfer the body to the quilt. The rigor mortis is gone, and they are careful and tender. They wrap the body completely and tie the quilt around and around with wide ribbon. Then they carry it out.

The road grader approaches, blading the dust and gravel washboard ridges, as the cortege is crossing. The driver raises the blade and steers the belching, roaring machine to the edge, diesel fumes dissipating into the pine tree branches.

"How long's this gonna hold us up?" the helper asks the driver.

"Not long." The driver peers at the town hall doorway, estimating the size of the crowd. "Not all that many of them."

"Who died, anyway?"

"Some drunk Indian. Laid on the railroad tracks in the Cities got hisself run over."

The open grave is rectangular the first four feet down, then it becomes oval. The difference furnishes a ledge. The draped body is lowered into the oval aperture, the feet at the west.

Simon prays in Indian, wishing Archie a good journey, asking the spirits to receive him, asking the Loon Clan spirits especially to be kind and helpful to him. He puts down semas and turns away, and others step up to put down their tobacco too.

One Johnson boy climbs back into the grave, standing on the rectangle ledge above the oval, and the others hand down the two-foot-long popple logs that are laid, one next to the other, on the ledge until they completely cover the oval part of the grave. When it is done, he climbs out and they start tossing in the dirt.

Everything is neat, every last scrap of leftover dirt raked atop the little mound. Then they place the grave house on top. It is made of unpainted pine boards and has a gable roof. At the west end wall a little window has been cut, and there is a tiny sill. A small plate of feast food is put there, nourishment for the spirit on its journey.

Old Peter is watching closely, David at his elbow.

When every last detail has been tended, checked, and checked again, they set the dodaim pole with the loon figure at the foot of the grave. Archie has gone west.

THE PAINT JOB

I miss Uncle Henry," the little girl said, eyes misty. Old Howard was nonplussed. This son had been dead nearly two years of a pulmonary virus that defied the young doctors at the Indian hospital. It had taken a long time to diagnose. Eventually they even knew where he had picked it up, doing day work at a farm taking down an old barn where the virus thrived in dusty bat droppings. By then it was too late, and they knew that had they diagnosed it earlier, they still would not have been able to save the once husky young man. Howard looked at his little granddaughter, wondering what to say to her. By rights one did not speak of the dead; it was a wise old tradition that kept you from wallowing in grief—once you'd done your grieving it was over with—and it was a spiritual protection as well. Talk too much about someone gone west, their spirits might think they were needed back here, and this disturbed their rightful, earned respite in the spirit world.

"He was a good man, "Howard finally compromised. He took the little girl's hand in his huge gnarled paw. How sweet, how beautiful. He rejoiced in the universal childhood beauty and innocence.

"Come on, Kew, let's do something nice." She'd been named Susie, like his wife, but that had become Susie Q, then the Q became Kew, and now no one called her anything else.

"Holy shit!" Kew's older brother shouted from the front yard. Jazz was eleven to her eight.

Howard and Kew walked to the front door, the girl curious and Howard disapproving of the language; he had no need for expletives.

49

Parked in front of the modest frame bungalow was the shiniest Waldorf-converted 12-passenger van ever, brand new, and loaded with people. It was a subdued maroon with brilliant, intricate silver racing stripes and decals.

"Lookit the decals!" Jazz was circling the wonder, admiring the steel wire hubcaps, the brilliant hood ornament. His buddy Fred collected hood ornaments and had 59; this one would make it an even 60.

"How are you son?" The emerging man wore a starched white shirt, tie, and was slipping on a suitcoat. Another white man was getting out also pulling on a dark suitcoat. "What's your name, little boy?"

Jazz didn't like that, didn't like the little boy, the patronizing. *My name's Charles and they called me Chaz and that turned into Jazz* but he didn't say anything. He felt awkwardness and contempt, turned away and walked toward his grandfather in the doorway, standing nearby but not too close. He was too big to need protection.

The two suited men, Bibles in hand, approached. "Good morning," the first one said unctuously, a Uriah Heep in vestment-like black. "The blessings of the Lord upon you."

Howard glanced at the clear sky, the ancient pines in his yard, his pristine vegetable garden and Susie's flower beds, at the grandchildren, and nodded. "A beautiful day."

Susie, drawn by the commotion, was in the living room nearby but out of sight.

It was the second man who said, "We have come to share The Word. Have these children been bathed in the blood of the lamb?"

Howard gaped, Jazz made a face, Kew mumbled, "Ish!" and Susie exploded onto the front stoop. "That's disgusting! That's the most disgusting thing I ever heard!" She grabbed Kew's hand and hauled her inside the house.

"What I meant was . . . "

The first one interrupted, "Are these your children?"

"Grandchildren." Howard had an army of them and some were always coming to stay a day or two, a week or two, or longer. Everyone lived within walking distance and while Howard and Susie chafed at the mess, they felt empty when no one was camping out with them.

"We heard you were the Chief around here, so we wanted to talk with you," the first one continued, ignoring Howard's reply, barreling on. "We want to spend a few days here on the reservation, spread the Gospel and do good works. We have all these young people with us willing to work hard, help out, show and teach these people." The subtle emphasis on "these" made plain the separation, the distancing between the saved missionaries and the lost sheep Indians who were almost beyond salvation but for The Word and Good Deeds.

Howard had noticed the earnest young people filling the van, the boys in white shirts, ties, and dark suits, the girls in high-necked blouses and probably long skirts. Now that might be a good example to the youngsters, he thought, but Jazz, fingering his sideways baseball cap and hitching up baggy jeans, whispered, "Crazy. Girls wearing hats, boys no caps or nothing!" Jazz had sidled closer, wanting to miss nothing but not wanting to appear too interested or too involved.

"About being Chief and helping us," the first one pursued, and Howard was in another bind. It was just plain rude to contradict someone, even a white missionary seemingly deaf to nonverbal communication. Couldn't this intruder descending from his swank and gilded chariot tell that Howard's answer was no, he was no chief, whatever being a so-called chief was anyhow? Couldn't the missionary discern a negative from body language, from a reluctance to say the impolite word? Apparently not.

Susie had no constraints saying no in plain, simple language. She avoided it, but when push came to shove she spoke her mind. Howard was more old-fashioned, indirect at best, or letting someone go their own way even if it was wrong, letting them find out for themselves by their mistakes. To Howard the human way of communicating was by acquiring understanding rather than by stating the facts. Howard couldn't help it if these people lacked humanness.

The first missionary was staring at Howard's bedroom slippers, staring hard, taken somehow by the old man's wearing them outdoors in the middle of the day as though he was too lazy to put on shoes. An example of sloth, a mortal sin. Howard had trouble with his feet swelling, he was a big man and carried plenty of weight, and slippers or equally shopworn tennis shoes were comfortable. The missionary didn't ask, Howard didn't volunteer. Their respective unstated conclusions were that Howard was just another lazy Indian, the missionary rude and not a complete human.

"Well, I've lived here a long time," Howard tried to find a comfort level without lying. "I don't hold any office or anything like that. Just an old-timer, I guess."

The missionary tore his eyes away from the dilapidated slippers: "That's OK, Chief, we understand. Maybe if you could just let people know we'll be around a few days and willing to do good works, spread the Word."

Howard gave that a mild shrug and expressed the thought that by now "most people know you're around. Nice wagon you've got there. Real nice." Howard thought the whole family could fit in it going to powwows. He loved doing that, he and Susie sitting in folding chairs in front of the bleachers, some of the kids and grandchildren out in the ring dancing.

"Missionary Board bought it for us, it was expensive but it's doing the work of the Lord, so that made it all right. We don't hold much with luxuries, but this is for a good purpose."

Susie, overhearing all this in the house, spluttered, and Jazz ate the whole van with his eyes. "Racing stripes! Grampa, d'you see that!"

The missionary allowed himself a small smile. "The Waldorf conversion people donated all that. But, yes, it is very nice and we are proud of it."

Howard wanted to say something about pride being a sin, but kept it to himself.

Over the next three days the van made the rounds of the reservation, the missionaries visiting homes to spread The Word. After the initial visit to Howard the two adult leaders split, each accompanied by two or more earnest teenagers. At each house they left religious tracts and a flyer announcing a barbecue at the powwow grounds, everyone welcome.

The proffered food for the soul failed to evoke much response, but food for the stomach drew a full house. Everyone came, even the MediVan with elderly from the senior housing. The prayers were received politely and the food with gusto.

"Get me another plate of ribs, and corn?" Howard asked Jazz, but the boy was running off and did not hear.

"I'll get it," Susie said, Kew trailing along for seconds of chocolate cake.

Just as they returned with the food, the senior missionary took to the airwaves, holding the microphone close to his mouth.

"Folks, we want to thank you for the warm reception and hospitality we have received here," he intoned, "so we are going to stay an extra day or two and do some work for the community. We are going to do a cleanup at the cemetery. Anybody wants to can join us there tomorrow morning. And now let us give thanks to the Lord for the food and the fellowship."

"Anybody ask them to do that?" Susie was looking at Howard. He shook his head no.

"I suppose it won't hurt," Susie allowed. "Hope they don't bother the grave houses."

Howard looked worried but remained silent.

He woke early on the morrow, as usual, but it was midmorning before Kew and Jazz were up, dressed, and breakfasted. The three found the old cemetery swarming. The whole crew was there in their white shirts and blouses, but without jackets and ties. The place had been mowed and raked, tufts of grass clipped, and now the old grave houses were being repaired. The wood structures, about two feet by six and eighteen inches high, had little gable roofs. They were weathered to a silvery sheen, and on the older ones, roofs and some walls had given way. Moss grew on some of the cedar shake shingles.

"It's a shame those grave houses are falling in," the first missionary said loudly as he approached Howard. "We've never seen this custom you have of building houses over the graves, but we purchased lumber and paint and are fixing them. Most are just crumbling, half caved in."

"Oh Grampa, look, Uncle Henry's is painted white with green trim!" Kew ran over for a closer look. "It's pretty, just like a doll house!"

"They have little holes on one end," the missionary remarked.

Howard was so upset he spoke before thinking. "For the food offering on their spirit journey."

"That's funny," the man chuckled. "The dead can't eat."

"They can't smell the flowers you put out," Howard snapped and walked away.

"What's wrong, Grampa?" Jazz hung close.

"Sit down, boy." They found a downed tree on the edge of the grounds. "We don't paint or fix these grave houses because it's all supposed to return to nature, to where we and everything came from. The bones of the ancestors, they become part of the earth that gives us life, just like their teachings, their spirits, give us life, show us how to live. D'you understand?"

Jazz looked at his elder a while and then nodded.

"Good. It's a teaching you should remember."

Jazz watched the hammering and painting. "Shouldn't you stop them, Grampa? Explain it?"

"They didn't ask for explanation," Howard said in his slow way, over his anger now. "Besides, they'll be gone tomorrow, and give it a couple of winters and the paint'll be gone. In time the grave houses will go in the ground."

Howard looked as though there was more to say and Jazz waited. "Then too, these people are better at talking than listening. It makes me feel good you ask questions, listen to the answers."

By nightfall the work was done, all debris removed, the remodeled grave houses painted shiny white with green trim, noticeable from the road and a long ways away. No modest screening of brush and young trees remained. The old privacy was gone. Howard was still sitting on the log, watching the missionaries gather their tools and leave, the two men bringing up the rear. Howard heard them.

"A shame and a disgrace to let these odd little houses fall into neglect. Shows a lack of respect. Pagans, really."

"Without the Word and the Way of the Lord, there is only sloth and sin. We have done a good deed here, whether they appreciate it or not. We can but try. Perhaps in time our example will save their souls."

By the time Howard got home Susie had heard all about it. So had everyone else in the community. She took one look at her husband's face, changed her mind about saying anything, and set a plate of food before him. He ate dutifully, silently, and left.

Next morning the missionaries were at Howard's door as he ate breakfast and he rose to meet them at the stoop. The loaded van stood in front. Both missionaries were in full regalia, starched white shirts, nondescript ties, dark suits. They looked as though they wanted to speak but no words would come.

"What . . . what . . . " the older of the two finally stammered.

"We wanted to repay your hard work, your kindness and respect," Howard said gently. "You know, reciprocate."

The entire van had been painted fluorescent blaze orange.

ABSOLUTION

Phoebe walked a tightrope 300 miles long. It stretched from the remote corner of the reservation to the Twin Cities and you could never tell at which end you'd find her. If she wasn't at one or the other she was in transit.

"Gone again," says Maggie, walking the road to the little grocery with her friend Sally as they pass Phoebe's desolate two-bedroomer.

"She was here a while ago," says Sally. "I seen Father Fustian coming out."

Maggie says nothing and shows nothing. She has learned to keep her disapprovals subsurface.

Maggie has a pleasant face undisguised by the glasses and full helmet of slightly curling hair. Next to her, Sally looks positively huge.

"Went to see her when I was in the Cities last fall," Sally goes on nonstop. "She'd been drinking and was out, neighbors taking care of the kids. Didn't catch up with her."

Maggie walks on saying nothing. What's to be said?

"Pitiful. Then she comes home, goes t'church hanging on the priest's frock like a kid to her mom's skirt," Sally is saying.

Not always, Maggie is thinking as Sally talks on.

"Lets go a'the Father t'go see the doctor. Always ailin', gettin' pills. Then gone again. See her whenever. Pitiful. Used t'be brightest kid in my mission school class. Beautiful handwriting, and pretty, my, when she was confirmed, I still remember how she looked.

Maggie looks stolid, expressionless; few people guess at the intensity of her emotions.

"How come you never helped her?" Sally pursues. "You're grand medicine, you heal people? 'Sides, you used to drink, you know what that's like, you been straight and it's going good for you. How many years now?"

"Going on seven."

"So how come you never, you know, did a healing?"

"People got to ask, got to really want it, bring tobacco."

It wouldn't be right to tell, it'd be for Phoebe to say she had brought tobacco, had asked to be taught how to walk the Red Road; talk about other people coming to you, you lose the power.

"Full moon tonight," Maggie says. "It's the time for woman's renewal, for celebrating the magic, the mystery of life-giving power. The time for the women to gather around the outdoor fire, praying to Grandmother Moon for strength and support, praying for other women like daughters, sisters, mothers, friends. Time for giving thanks for the water without which there would be no life, for the water in which the unborn fruit to birth, for the water which is the woman's special responsibility to keep clean, to protect, to offer to the men at ceremonies just like the men have to care for the fire. Hope Ralph'll be around tonight to make the fire; a man has to do that. But for sure, he always seemed to know when it was time. And she'd have to be sure to get some more cloth at the store to offer Grandmother Moon on behalf of all the women, raising it in her hand at the end of the prayer, then letting it lower, dipping one corner into the flames until the whole yard of it began to burn, and dropping it into the fire for all of it to burn, saying migwetch, thank you, cleanse me, cleanse all of us, renew us, renew our womanhood power.

They would be circling the fire, each taking a turn at the west facing the east-rising moon to pray and offer cloth, moving clockwise around the blaze like daylight travels clockwise from sunrise to sunset to sunrise again. Saying prayers for the ones beaten, for the little ones used in a bad way by grown-ups, for the old ones living in loneliness and neglect. Saying thanks, always thanks, for the good, for life, for creation, for womanhood.

"Got to be someplace tonight," Sally says. Sally's always got to be elsewhere on moon ceremony night, flirting with the Red Road through her friendship with Maggie, but avoiding involvement like a kid dipping toes into a cold lake and going home with a dry towel.

Maggie lets it go. When she's ready, she'll come, she thinks. Like Phoebe did last fall and winter, wanting to learn how to walk in beauty, in spiritual balance with everything around her. Even when bad things were happening you could feel all in one piece inside of you, that's where the Red Road led east to west. It was when the Black Road north to south took over, that road of everyone out for theirselves, and there was no Red Road to balance it, that people got lost.

Phoebe had come into their house and sat at the kitchen table, and Ralph had taken one look and gone out to work on the woodpile, knowing the women needed to talk privately.

"I want what you got," Phoebe had said and started to cry, her face still half pretty but showing dissolution, the edema of alcohol. "I can't go on like this."

Maggie waited.

"Am I supposed to give tobacco?" Phoebe fumbled in her purse for a cigarette and offered it. "Is this all right?"

Maggie raised the cigarette in her left hand and palmed it. "It's semas. It'll be offered for you, cause you gave it. The spirits'll know it's your semas. Next time get a package of pipe tobacco, that'll be good."

"I'm broke," Phoebe said.

Maggie said nothing. What's to be said? That she had enough money for booze, for cigarettes, she could surely find a dollar, dollar and a half, for tobacco? That she could learn how to make the real thing from inner red willow bark? That it'd mean more if her own hands had made it than if she'd bought it at the store?

"You'll find a way," Maggie said. "What's troubling you?"

Phoebe's jaw muscles clenched and her face puffed up, her being swelled like having lockjaw while her insides yeasted and boiled. She struggled and spasmed a long time but when the words finally erupted it was a volcano spewing quicksilver, bits and pieces bouncing all over making no coherent sense except for the pain, the awful contorted pain of a rubber man twisted and tied in unravelable knots, twisting his head this way and that, wiggling fingers and toes but unable to get free; a shaman tied in a shaking tent who's lost his power to escape the bonds and just stays that way forever.

"... come home and no job then they lost my papers at welfare and no check and the kids in trouble in school so we went back t'the Cities. An' that Chuck brings home this young feller and made me do it with him and took Polaroids, I know he did but I was half out of it then 'cause I saw th' flash. One time he did the daughter he must of thought I was all the way gone well I knew I could see but I was like paralyzed couldn't move couldn't talk she cried I know I heard that. This man at charities he said he didn't have nothin' t'give, you know no food, but if I did this thing to him maybe he could find something so I done it."

Maggie listened and watched and felt the pain.

"Come home Father Fustian says I got to find Jesus, pray the Lord an' go confess. I did too. But he says I know it was him sittin' behind that thing he's the only one, he says I don't really mean it 'cause I been there before so often an' he can't absolve, you know forgive, if he don't think I mean it . . . so I mean, what the hell . . . "

Then the wracking sobs came from so far down, from so deep in Phoebe that all Maggie could do was to sit quietly and wait.

"I don't want that booze and that dope, that poison. I want t'be a good mom, I love those kids . . . "

Maggie waited while more of the pain came out.

Anger stopped the catharsis. "I was confirmed, damn him, I been t'mass. I eat that wafer while he swills th'wine. I know he's suppose t'forgive, that's what they taught, God forgives . . . " More gasps and sobs and her throat was raw. "I don't know. It's all so fakey, so playing at it, games. They say the old people, they never had this kind of shit life. Me, I don't even know how t'talk Indian, just some words. I don't remember nothin' from when I was little, hardly nobody talked Indian in our house, just when they didn't want me t'know what they was talking about. And the nuns always saying: now don't be Indianish little girl. Ish. I know what that means in Indian. Means bad. What do you do in a sweat?"

Ralph had built the fire to heat the rocks in his usual careful way, fussing with the first four chunks of firewood to lay out an exact square, putting a bit of each of the four sacred medicines in the middle after holding them up in a gesture of offering and saying a silent prayer. Then came the wigwas, the birchbark, and on top of the square, four logs to make a platform.

"How many rocks d'you say?" he called over to Maggie, who was neatening the inside of the dome-shaped sweat lodge.

"Eh?" She stuck her head out the doorway opening, the tarp folded up.

"How many?"

"Seventeen."

"Just women you said, not even one man?" Usually at least one man was asked into a women's sweat, reaffirming that it takes the joining of man and woman to shelter, shield, succor a family, to make life complete, just as the bent poles—one from each side tied together at the top—represented the union of man and woman for the completion of life. Maggie had given him tobacco to make the fire and be ashkabewis, helper, who hands in the rocks and closes the flap. They had done this hundreds of times, but even so they offered the tobacco when asking each other to do a spiritual task.

"That's right," she said without explaining, and Ralph figured the newcomer had some special woman problems that were none of his business, not that it took much guesswork to know that Phoebe was carrying a heavy load of some kind.

He picked the rocks from the pile they hauled twice a year and pyramided them on the platform, and then stood split logs on end all around the square. It looked like the picture of a small Maya temple. Ralph left an opening in front, the east side, which he stuffed with more wigwas, twigs, and kindling. It was ready to light an hour, hour and a half before they were ready to go in. He'd know the time because Maggie would do the newcomers' teaching after they all showed and that always took a while.

They began to arrive while the sun was still up, still showing above the tree tops but sinking. It was a yellowy, glittery closing of daylight that would turn red and then purple, but right now it cast creation in   golden iridescence. They came dressed in jeans, some in dresses, carrying towels and other necessaries. Maggie had told Phoebe not to worry about not having a cotton shift that would hang loose and be comfortable in the sweat, she had an extra that would fit. The women sat on folding chairs and stumps scattered near the riverbank, a patch about twenty feet from the lodge that had come to be a little lounging area by usage and common consent. You could see the house through the trees but not the road, and the trees and brush shielded the area from dust, noise, and passersby. Each woman as she arrived would wave at the others, say, "Boojoo" or "Aneen," and go down to the riverbank to offer tobacco and prayers before joining the others to chat about weather, kids, and other commonplace concerns of the day.

"Waiting for Ruth and Sarah," Maggie said. "Said they'd be here."

"Maybe they're on Indian time," somebody said and they all laughed, although they knew Maggie liked to start her sweats at sundown, saying it was the best time because that's when the spirits started to come out, that it was a bugonageshik, a hole in the sky, one of three each day when the smoke of the offerings most readily ascended to the spirits.

Ralph had lit the wigwas when the first car pulled into the yard, and one wooden match was enough to get the pyramid ablaze. It worked that way summer and winter, rain, shine or snow if you built it all the right way, and Ralph knew that as soon as the last two arrived Maggie would say, "Now this is a sacred fire and we don't throw butts or paper or gum wrappers in there. Use the coffee can over there for trash." They all knew it except it was a nice way to inform a newcomer.

When the last ones arrived they changed into their cotton dresses or shifts over behind the big trees, draped the towels over their necks, and came around behind the lodge. They put out their tobacco, a little into the fire which was really hot and burning down now, cherry red rocks peeking through the remaining wood, and they put the rest on the rock altar in the center of the crescent-shaped mound within whose arms the rocks were being heated.

"It's shaped like Grandmother Moon in a crescent," Maggie began the ancient teaching, "and we got this trail of cedar branches all around it and leading into the lodge to show how we were given the sweat lodge long ago . . . "

They stood while she told it, about the Little Boy and the long fast and the healing cedar. They'd all heard it many times except for Phoebe who inhaled every word, who quit worrying for the first time that day about how hot it would be in the sweat and would she be able to take it and would there be some scary things happening and

. . . this sounded so sweet, so wholesome, and Phoebe started feeling better.

"So that's how the sweat lodge was given to the Ahnishinabeg long, long ago," Maggie was saying in her dreamy sing-songy voice that she fell into when doing a teaching, remembering the oral tradition. "And when we go into the lodge we go on the left and after we come out on the right. Clockwise. And we go on our hands and knees like little babies, because it's like being reborn, and the water and steam in there is like the water around a baby in the mother's belly, and the lodge is like the womb, even shaped like it, except half of it is below the ground where we can't see it t'remind us we can never know it all, only some of it, because we're just human, Ahnishinabeg, and only the Creator, Gitchie Manidoo, knows it all. OK, let's line up. Rocks ready? Bessie, you sit west door, hold the shaker and put the cedar on the rocks when they come in. Sarah, you sit south. Phoebe, you come right next to me and Ruth next to you."

When they were all inside, seated in a circle around the shallow pit that was ready for the rocks, Maggie called for Ralph to hand in the hand drum, cedar bowl, and other paraphernalia.

"You got any ear rings or other metal on you?" Maggie asked Phoebe. "I forgot to ask before, better take them off, hand them out. Ralph'll keep 'em for you. OK Ralph, ready for the grandfathers. Four. Then the pipe. Then three more an' you can close it."

Bertha sat east door, just left of the opening, and used the deer antlers to pick up the glowing red rocks as Ralph slid them in on the pitchfork. He was fastidious about brushing off coals and cinders, but once in a while some small bits of charcoal that had caught between the rock and a pitchfork tine fell, and Maggie picked them up with her fingers and tossed them out while Bertha lifted the rock into the pit. Bertha arranged the first four rocks, one for each direction, and Bessie placed a tiny sprig of cedar on each, which sputtered and crackled, the tiny sparks fading to ash in moments.

"Boojoo, Mishomis," the women muttered greeting as each rock came into the little cave of the lodge, "hello, Grandfather."

They had a pipe, passing it clockwise for each to draw smoke and handed it out to Ralph, who knelt in the opening and smoked it too. Then Maggie prayed in Indian, giving thanks for the sacred medicines, all the creatures on earth, the water, the skies, and sang in Indian keeping time on her hand drum while Bessie kept time with the shaker. Most of the women sang along.

"That was asking the spirits not to be shy, to come in and be with us," Maggie explained. "Three more, Ralph."

After the rocks he handed in the pail of water and the dipper. Then the flap was closed.

"A little light coming in under the door," Maggie tapped on the tarp to show where. "That's good now. See, Phoebe, it's got to be dark all the way in here. Now there's nothing t'be scared of, only good happens in here. If it gets hot, you can put the washcloth over your face and breathe through that, or slide down 'cause it's hotter up high than down low. Gets a little too hot, try praying for others who're in more pain than you are, people in hospitals and nursing homes, women getting beaten. Gets to be too much, tell me and we'll open the door, cool it off a while."

Maggie poured a dipper of water over the rocks and instant steam rose and enveloped them. She sang again and prayed. Then it was Bertha's turn to pray. She was a wisp of a woman in her 50s, older by ten or twenty years than the rest, and she did her ritual thanksgiving and praying for others.

"I'm sorry, Grandfathers, to have to use the borrowed language but my Indian's not so good. I want to say migwetch, thanks, for my sobriety. I don't know no Indian word for sobriety, maybe because there didn't used to be any booze among us Indians back in the old days. Anyway, I'm thankful not to be that way any more. This Red Road is a good way to walk, it's brought me peace and good feelings. My kids come visit, they don't have to worry bringing their little ones to visit Grandma. It didn't used to be that way."

As Bertha recalled episodes from her younger years, Phoebe began to sob. It started with tears leaking down her face and graduated to the real thing, that emptying of old pain which comes from deep in the chest below the sternum, not that holding back kind of rasping in the back of the throat. Bertha kept on talking, Bessie felt around for the twist of sweetgrass and held one end against one of the grandfathers until it ignited, sending the sweet smell intermixed with the steam, the sweetness to drive the badness away, and Maggie sang softly in Indian, thumping muted time on her hand drum.

It went around to each of the women in turn, and each talked about her life, her pain, her surmounting her past, and the beauty of life. Each prayed thanks for the grandeur of creation of which each is a part. When it came to Bessie, she said, "It's to the west door," and Maggie signaled Ralph to open the flap.

In the darkening outside it had cooled, and it felt good to Phoebe to suck in the drier night air.

"D'you hear the wolves singing?" Ralph asked. "Over across the river a ways."

Nobody had, but Ruth and Sarah both said they'd felt a draft across their faces and over their shoulders during the praying. "Like a bird flying by."

"Maybe Migizi was with us," Maggie said. "Nobody too hot? Too uncomfortable?"

They were all sweating, the cotton shifts soaked, but it was all right, even for the newcomer.

"Let's go on. OK, Ralph, rest of the rocks."

It was hotter now and with the flap down, Maggie started a new song. "Aahhh . . . shkabaywis . . ." they all sang, and Ralph outside felt tears coming to his eyes at the same time the half smile came to his lips. They were singing thanks to him for being ashkabaywis, being helper.

When it came around to Phoebe she didn't know what to say. "I got all these feelings, but I got no words," she finally managed.

"That's all right," Maggie said, "the grandfathers know what's in your heart. They know it even if we don't say it out loud. And we're forgiven for mistakes when we don't know better, we never been taught. The Creator knows we're just human, we make mistakes. We fall down, the eagle feather catches us, helps us back up. I'll do that teaching some time."

Phoebe felt weak-kneed after they crawled out of the lodge and she tried to stand up. She noticed most of the women sat on the ground, cooling off gradually. Ralph was nowhere to be seen; he had raked the fire embers together and put a few more logs on to revive the blaze, then disappeared in respect for their modesty.

"Clear night," Ruth said, "feels like there should be northern lights. How you feel, Phoebe?"

"Good, I feel so good. I'm so grateful you let me come."

"This way is here for anybody wants to walk it," Maggie said. "It don't belong to any one person, it's here for all us Indian people. Anybody, really. It's to share."

Three days later Maggie was walking the road past Phoebe's house on the way to get milk and bread at the store and heard the shrill piping voice coming out the door which had been left ajar.

"Filthy, evil pagan rite! It's the devil's work!" It was Father Fustian. "You're a lost soul, you're damned! That's what you are. You're headed for eternal hellfire. I heard you went in that Indian sweat, you of all people, mission school trained and confirmed, and now look at you! Backsliding pagan!"

"I'm sorry, Father, I'm sorry, I don't want to go to hell," Phoebe pleaded. "Come back, Father. Please come back. Father. Please."

But the little man stormed out, his splotchy pate ringed by reddish fringe, cassock skirt floating behind him.

Maggie kept on walking. It was for Phoebe to sort out where she wanted to be.

The next day Father Fustian was back. Maggie saw his car but this time the door was shut.

Then the house was closed and Phoebe was gone.

Sally and Maggie are walking home from the store.

"How long's she been gone?" Sally asks as they pass Phoebe's.

"Most a week, I think."

"Ain't seen her since that priest was here." Sally marches along. "Five days. Hey, where you going?"

Maggie detours to Phoebe's locked door. She peers through the windows but the shades are pulled down tightly as always when Phoebe is at the other end of the tightrope. Maggie sets her grocery bags down on the front steps and walks around to the back.

She is gone a long time and Sally begins to fret, feeling funny standing by the side of the road with her groceries, just hanging out in front of Phoebe's. Then Maggie comes out the front door looking awful and the evil smell follows her.

"What's wrong, Maggie? What's the matter?"

Maggie is gagging and retching by the roadside but nothing comes up. "She's been dead all this time. Bottle a' hospital pills empty by th' bed."

Father Fustian doesn't allow use of the cemetery next to the church because it is consecrated ground, but after the four-day wake in the community hall which he boycotts, he is persuaded to come to the Indian cemetery to conduct the burial. The medicine men who do funerals are all unavailable; one is in Canada, another visiting friends, and the task goes to Fustian by default. Everyone can see his engineer boots and the rolled-up pants because the cassock is too short to hide them and waves in the wind at graveside

There is quite a crowd and as it gathers around the excavation ringed by new dirt Father Fustian again frets about the sorry state of the place. The old grave houses are collapsing, disintegrating, and there are no gravestones or markers. Can never teach these Indians anything.

He reads the service out of his dog-eared manual and signals that the casket can be lowered.

"You can come up here for a blessing before you go home," he says, but nobody moves.

Maggie walks to the open grave and takes some semas from her tobacco pouch. She holds it to the sky and prays aloud in Indian: "Migwetch for the earth, all of it. For every rock, tree, every grain of sand, for the trees and the flowers, for the sky and the water. Migwetch for those that fly, that crawl, swim and those who walk. Migwetch for life, for the sacred medicines, for the eagle that flies over us to see how we walk. Help us deal with our grief in the proper way, to show our respect. Help us in those times when we want to help other people and don't know how."

She drops her arm and sprinkles the semas on the casket and walks away, avoiding the waiting priest. One after another the others file by, putting down their semas, bypassing Father Fustian and walking away.

The young men of the family wait until last to make their offering before shoveling in the earth. They work quietly until it is done, tamped, and the loose stuff raked. Tomorrow they will bring out a grave house to put over the burial site, and it will not be labeled or repaired over the years but allowed to rejoin the earth and become part of it, because that is the way it is said to do when you walk the Red Road.

When the women gather at the next full moon and the turn comes to Maggie, all she says about it is "Migwetch for the earth, it's all sacred, every bit of it, and so is the life you let us have, it's sacred too, every bit of it."

LUPUS! LUPUS!

At a distance the animal loping across the highway seems the size of a small deer. Can't be, Doc Brandt thinks, fussing with his ill-fitting glasses, vowing once again to schedule a new exam and get a better pair. Doesn't look right. A brush wolf? A timber wolf?

He likes to see wolves, the sightings few and far between but always exhilarating. It isn't just the beauty, the grace of the animal. There is a deep racial imprint, locked in legends of Nanabozho's wolf-brother who helps the Ojibwe folk hero hunt for food, the mutual respect between hunting partners. People who survived and flourished over millennia through hunting skill, endurance, and courage respect these qualities in others. Doc never thinks about it consciously; he just feels good seeing a wolf.

If Doc ever spends mental energy on the old teachings, it is about his own dodaimic linkage. His clan is loon, inherited from his father, and as a boy it was often told him by uncles and the grandfather that Loon Clan had special duties. "We're leaders but we're more," they would say. "We're healers between people, we bring peace. That's because loons are birds can fly in the air, relate to the wind, the other birds, and loons can swim under water and relate to the water manidoos. Only clan can do both." The sense of dodaimic identity has given Doc strength and comfort all his life.

Curious, he speeds down the concrete ribbon flanked by deep ditches to catch the northwoods runoff. Patches of pine and peat bog covered with Indian tea plants flit past until he slows at about the

69

place of the crossing. He thinks he has missed it when he sees the mountain lion on the embankment in profile. It is tawny and winter-thin, ribs showing, and disappears into the brush.

"Panther! Never seen one! Born, raised here, practiced medicine a lifetime, travelled every road, and never seen one!" Doc gave himself permission to talk aloud to himself long ago, a solacing companionship on solitary drives. He knows the sighting will have to stay secret with him; if the story got out, some trapper or bushwhacker would be after it just to be able to say nonchalantly, "I got that there panther the other day."

That's what happened the time he saw the fisher, a mature animal in prime, its long sable-like fur glistening in the sun as it skittered down the diagonal trunk of a fallen tree and slipped into a creek. Doc had been sitting on the bank, taking a few minutes to enjoy the day on his way from here to there, and the fisher had not seen or scented him.

"Five feet long if an inch, and half of it the tail," he had said at the coffeeshop, still marveling. Sure enough, a few weeks later someone had trapped it. Fisher were rare now, vicious when hunting squirrels in the trees, or porcupines, but very dumb. Just set a trap on a leaning tree used as runway, and wait. Same kind of set as used for bobcat. He would keep quiet this time.

He has seen timber wolves, deer, fox, and much other wildlife along the lonely highways. This stretch is devoid of even crossroads, a forty-mile causeway through wilderness that even Indians in the old days avoided except when tracking game or gathering medicines.

Nowadays any degree of Indian parentage makes one Indian, but Doc is old and in his youth he was considered half-breed, a good example for whites to point to as he struggled through Carlisle Indian Institute and Johns Hopkins. A Good Indian, see, not like this riffraff. He was honored to his face and called Our Own Medicine Man behind his back by whites, the first Indian M.D. in the state. He knew it, ignored it, but it still rankled.

Indians on the nearby reservations went to the public health clinics for the dailies, sometimes to the few dispensers of old-time herbal medicines, but in a pinch visited Doc. He would lean back and listen, feel and thump when necessary, talk old-time medicine about which he had learned a little as a boy from his grandmother (and more as an adult, reconciling the digitalis of prescriptions with foxglove, and coming to respect the old empirical wisdom). He had come to accept his Spartan, lonely role, to accept the ironies of life and human mindsets, and to prefer his solitariness.

The long stretch of wild country ends temporarily and he parks at the combination bar, restaurant, filling station, and sawmill fifteen miles north of where the panther had crossed. He ambles in.

"Been a while, Doc," Ben Miller greets him. "Up to check your Aunt Emma's old place?"

"Last time, I hope," Doc says. "Coffee. Yeah, I think it's finally sold."

"About time. Who's the new neighbor?"

"Haven't met him. It's all by correspondence. Some monk or priest is all I know."

"That's all we need, some religious nut. Holy Rollers," the voice explodes from the side of the room, hostile, angry.

"Sounds like Rich Johnson," Doc squints over. "Lovely as always. Might do you some good to have a priest living around here. Keep you from shining deer and getting into trouble."

"Never mind the deer," Johnson parries. "Bring your cup over. Keep us company. Looks like it's company day for our little town."

"Little town is a joke and we all know it," Doc balances the cup as he steps carefully over the uneven plank floor. "Fishbone isn't a town, it's a state of mind."

"So long as we're incorporated we get the lower taxes." Ben Miller squeezes his beer belly to the table. "Not to mention the liquor license."

"Only town in the state with one building and sixteen inhabitants."

"Fifteen, " Ben corrects. "Jesse moved to the Cities."

"Fifteen, and thirteen of them are scattered over two townships." Doc nods at the fourth man at the table, Deputy Sheriff Clem Stanley. He is about to ask Stanley what he is doing in Fishbone, but he knows.

Two or three times a year Stanley drives the distance to show the flag for law and order. He spends a few hours visiting. It was understood at the county seat and in Fishbone that some occasional poaching would be overlooked so long as the venison ended on the poacher's table and was not sold to disappointed city hunters. There were other irregularities around Fishbone having to do with breaches of trapping regulations and illegal netting of fish, and occasionally someone cut sawlogs on state land. The paucity of inhabitants and the relatively small scale of the derelictions virtually guaranteed immunity. There never were witnesses, complaints, if any, were old and evidence nonexistent.

True, there were rumors from time to time that Rich Johnson illegally trapped wolves and sold the pelts across the border in Canada, but no one had ever caught him. And there were suspicions that Ben Miller did his deer hunting a mite before the official season and that city hunters who boarded at his place never left empty-handed.

"Horse feathers," Ben once said when asked. "So many deer in these woods nobody should go empty-handed ever. You miss out last year? Come stay at my place you'll get one. Guaranteed."

It was an ambiguous reply. Yet one of Fishbone's folkways was that no one ever admitted anything, direct questions were ignored or side-stepped, but that it was all right to ask outsiders anything. At the county seat they spoke of Fishboners as jackpine savages or rednecks, and the unspoken attitude was that Fishbone was a good place to avoid unless you just had to go to or through it.

"Tell us about this religious nut that's coming here," Rich leans forward, his unshaven chin approaching Doc's coffee cup. His clothing smells of fuel oil, gasoline, and chain saw bar oil, a common Fishbone aroma.

"Can't say there's much to tell." Doc enjoys playing the Fishbone game right back, falling into a passive-aggressive role. He plays with his coffee cup and in the long silence schemes how to lure Ben and Mitch into asking more questions, into saying more than they otherwise would. He finally says, "Had a letter from my cousin out East in that monastery."

"You got a cousin in a monastery?" Ben Miller is surprised. "Didn't even know you was Catholic."

"I'm not. He's third or fourth cousin." Doc lets it sit there a while and then changes the subject. "Any more trouble with wolves? Lose any more livestock?"

"Damn wolves." Rich is off on a tirade, his hatred of wolves proverbial. "Got a heifer in that pasture back of the barn last year. This year a calf and two sheep. Don't pay t'keep turkeys. Damn government protecting them. Anything happens one of their wolves you got Fish and Wildlife over you like fleas on a dog, but they don't give a hoot in hell about our livestock."

"Maybe if you brought your stock in before calving and lambing you wouldn't be drawing those wolves," Doc said. "That smell of the afterbirth draws like bait. And when you butcher, well, you ought to bury your dead livestock and the leavings from butchering, not let it lie around. That's baiting wolves or coyotes. Like using a garbage dump to bait bears."

"Got nothing to do with it." Rich is defensive. "Not a thing. Any butchering leftovers or dead livestock go to feed the sled dogs anyhow, not much left lying around these days. About your Holy Rollers now, Doc. They gonna be a cult or something here? A whole bunch?"

"I doubt it." Doc glances at his watch. "Nearly seven miles to Aunt Emma's old place and I have to check it before the sale is final. I told them the shed roof is bad and there are some leaks in the house roof. The old priest said he would fix it."

"Priest?" Rich utters it as an expletive.

"You know, monk or priest," Doc says. "He's sick and wants solitude. Quiet. Some relative's coming to live in and take care of him. He wanted privacy, a private place, so you guys can quit worrying about having a Nosy Parker moving in. You go right ahead poaching and bootlegging wolf hides, he isn't likely to get in your way. He sounds too sick to be doing any soulsaving either, so you can forget about that too. I just hope when he needs an assist you'll help without overcharging too much."

"What d'you mean, poaching, bootlegging . . ." Rich leans forward again defensive-combative, but Ben Miller intercedes.

"We'll give him a hand, Doc. Privacy works two ways. He'll be coming for gas and groceries. We'll look out for him without bothering."

The whites who occupy Fishbone seem a collection of Jukes and Kalikaks to Doc, society's superstitious and dim-witted rejects who have come to like it that way. Ben at times seems to have some social graces, but Rich is more typical—surly, wily, proud of his ignorance and bitter toward those smarter, better educated, better off. His children would be reared and conditioned to be like him as he had been molded by his father.

"Suppose the old medicine man'll come look after the priest?" Doc hears Rich's reedy voice but he keeps walking to his car.

"Naw," Ben is saying. "He's just glad t'get rid of the place. An' you be polite t'the priest he gets here."

Doc has an uncomfortable feeling as he leaves. It has little to do with Fishboners. "They stick in my craw," Doc mumbles to himself. It's an indefinable something, a sense of imbalance, of something out of kilter, which he cannot place or define. On the drive home he sees nothing out of the ordinary.

"Fill 'er up, Father?" Ben asks.

"OK," he murmurs with averted head, "call me Theo. I'm not a priest. Nor a monk any more."

It is twilight going on dark and Ben cannot see his new neighbor clearly. The man's widebrimmed felt hat and upturned collar, his gray-ing beard, mask the face. He appears to be of middle height, judging from his posture in the driver's seat. The small patches of visible skin seem a sallow yellow and they twitch. He averts his head when the nervous tic comes upon him, and Ben thinks he sees weeping sores on the other cheek. Poor man, he thinks, and goes to pump gas. Maybe he has skin cancer.

The girl has gone to the store with a shopping list. She is a scrawny twelve-year-old, pale and furtive-eyed, not the stout, elderly house-keeper that Fishbone had expected.

"Anybody around here sell firewood?" Theo mumbles as he pays.

"Rich Johnson from time to time."

"Tell him four cords. Any evening next week. Cash." He doesn't ask how much a cord.

Rich'll like that, Ben thinks. Cash is nonexistent at tax time and Rich will certainly take additional advantage of the stranger's unfamiliarity with local charges for firewood. Back in the store he compares impressions with his wife.

"Kid's orphaned," she says. "Least her mother died. She didn't say nothing about a father. Priest's her uncle. Tutoring insteada school. Poor tyke all skinny 'n pale. Name's Lisa 'n she's doin' for him. What's he like?"

"Pretty sick if you ask me. Nervous twitchy an' sores. Won't look atcha like he don't want you t'see it. Sad."

Uncle and niece come once a week to buy foodstuff and odds and ends, the man staying in the car, the girl shopping, list in hand, neither saying much, both anxious to leave quickly, their visits always in the evening just before the store closes.

"Come in an' coffee?" Ben invites.

Theo shakes his head.

"Let us know you need anything," Ben says and the man mumbles thanks.

"Rich'll be out with the wood in a couple days," Ben goes on and Theo nods he has heard.

"Deliver wood t'the priest?" Ben asks a few days later when Rich comes in.

Rich nods. "Queer cuss. He opens the door a crack and screeches out at me t'come back in the evening like he told you. Real mad. So I made the second trip."

"What's the place like? They do anything to it?"

"Picked up real clean around the house. Patched the roof. That's about it. Sure an ugly cuss, ain't he? Walks hunched up more like, hobbles, you know."

"Never seen him walk," Ben answers. "He never gets out the car here. You sell him some a that good state wood?"

"Kind of hard telling where the line runs back in the brush like that. Could've sworn I was on my own land," Rich grins. "Wolves got a runway through that northeast popple island. Fresh tracks and hair sticking to the brush."

Both know the area and that when wolves shed in spring and autumn, hair from the ruffs catches on low-hanging branches. It is a sign for which trappers look.

That night the wolf pack howls, the ululating seeming to come from all points of the compass as the pack gathers at rendezvous. It can be clearly heard in the Fishbone Store where Ben and his wife look up at each other, say nothing, and go back to their preoccupations, he to the day-old newspaper, she to her solitaire. Rich Johnson hears it too. He pads out of his overheated cabin with its sleeping children and overtired wife into the cool still of the starry night. He eases the door shut and listens, trying to deduce the location of the rendezvous. Now that the pack has moved back, the wolves will use the same spot or spots to gather for hunting deer or moose, or for its social protocols. Rich knows wolves well. He knows that pack members stray and wander great distances for days and weeks at a time, but that the focus, the heart of the pack somehow stays glued together. If he can locate their rendezvous and major runways he might do very well. Canadian fur prices have finally gone up again and the black market should bring over $400 per pelt.

Where are they? He inches the door open, reaches backward for the felt-lined shoepacs, and shuts the door again. A solo wolf howl, two or three miles northwest. Answering howls from several directions.

He wishes that he dared to imitate the howling. Some people can "call" wolves and get them to respond, but he is self-conscious about trying it. The idea of howling like a wolf is stupid, disgusting. Sooner kill one than act like one, he thinks.

Time to drive the few gravel roads and logging trails, he decides. Drive, park, and listen. Make a box pattern around them and find out their home. Rich sets out patiently.

He finds himself near the priest's homestead and curiosity about the strange newcomer brushes aside his interest in the howling wolves, the single voice answered by the still-scattered pack. A stray trying to ingratiate himself in pack territory?

Never mind. What's Father Theo up to? He parks his truck at least a half-mile away. Rich glimpses a fluttering light in a window, like candlelight repeatedly shadowed by a death-drawn moth.

It is candlelight! The jerk doesn't even have electricity, Rich thinks. He walks quietly to the house and peers in the window but sees nothing save the sparse furniture in the spotless room. No one seems about. He walks softly around the corner, intending to look into a window on the opposite side of the clapboard house, when a wolf howls a few feet away.

Rich whirls in surprise, fright, and freezes. He has never known a wolf to be this close to a dwelling, or to humans, and stay around long enough to howl.

Again. "Aaaawhooooooo . . ."

Eerie. It comes from around the corner of the house.

Flat against the wall, Rich oozes to the corner and peers around the edge of the clapboards. His heart is pounding and his sweat has the stink of fear, but then adrenaline is mother's milk to Rich. His nostrils have widened as, animalistic himself, he is compelled to spy the beasts.

At the edge of the clearing, dim but still visible in the starlit night, it is prowling back and forth and howls yet again. There is no moonlight but the night is lucid.

Rich is rigid, frozen in disbelief as it sits on its haunches and once more gives voice. As it lifts its head to howl the teeth glisten in the faint illumination and fluoresce. Rich bolts and runs, heart pounding, sweat streaking into his eyes and burning there.

Werewolf!

All the superstitions and fears, all the children's scare stories and whisperings of the supernatural gather in Rich Johnson's gut; the adrenaline pumps, his body sprints, and his mind races. He trips, tumbles, sprawls on the ground and is stunned. The cold dampness of the turf helps him to collect his wits. Ridiculous. Rich Johnson, unafraid of the law or the woods, running from a fairy tale? He gets up, brushes off, and carefully retraces his steps.

Once again there is the candlelit window and the empty room. Once again he presses himself against the side wall and peers around the corner.

"Uncle Theo, come inside now," the scrawny little girl is saying. "It's late. I'm getting cold."

"A little longer. Just a little bit." Father Theo's voice is high-pitched and raw. Both figures are at the edge of the clearing where Rich had seen the wolf before, but he cannot make out what they are doing. The girl appears to be standing still, huddling into her coat or jacket. The monk is moving about, then moves a few steps closer to the house in his hobbling, awkward shuffle of a gait and begins to wail at the sky. It is a screeching chant that carries into the night air:

Lupus! Lupus!
Versipellis!
Est futurus
Verminellis.

Then:

> *Lupus! Lupus! Versipellis!*
> *Gravitar es maledictus, donum cutis*
> *mihi dabis, validae et integrae . . .*

He shrieks it over and over, stress pitching his voice ever higher, his hunchbacked posture exaggerating the length of his arms reaching upward, supplicating the dark skies.

Rich is terrified, his sweat-caked hair bristles. He does not understand the Latin chant but he senses an unspeakable horror.

"I'm scared, Uncle Theo," little Lisa shivers. "And I'm so cold! Please, can't we go in now?"

"It has to be done," he rasps, panting, gulping his breaths. "We must exorcise the curse."

"Can I go in? You come when you're done?"

"You must stay!" The voice rises to hysteria. "Stay! It's for you! It may be too late for me; I'm doing it more for you!"

"I don't know what you mean, Uncle Theo." She sounds such a little waif seeking to shrink further into her childhood.

"Your mother died of it and I am fading. Now you are showing the signs. Be still, child. It's done for you."

"Please, please . . . "

"All right. We'll try again another time."

They turn and step toward the house and Rich sees them clearly, his eyes adjusted to the starlit night, the figures away from the dark backdrop of the woods. The girl's sallow face contrasts to her dark hair and clothing and stands out. The monk, hunched, contorted, and bearded looms beside her. His lips are drawn back in a sneer . . . a snarl . . . and his teeth . . . his teeth . . . are like fangs and they glow!

Rich chokes a scream, recoils from the sight, and flees.

He inclines his head and goes out to the gas pump. Ben follows. It is how they consult on contraband.

"How many pelts?" Ben asks.

Rich shakes his head. "It's that priest." He pauses. "It's crazy. I don't know. I'll talk t'ya some other time."

Rich pivots, vaults into his pickup truck and drives off. Ben shrugs his shoulders and returns to wait on the trade.

The house in the woods draws Rich as a magnet attracts metal filings. In his thoughts he calls it The Werewolf Place. He has not seen man or girl outside but glimpses them at times moving about in the house. She usually sits quietly in an easy chair in a corner folded into herself; he is in another room.

This evening Rich hears them. It is warmer and a window has been cracked.

"Getting worse, isn't it?"

"I don't know, Uncle Theo. I suppose so."

"Eyes are getting worse, you can't stand to go outside in daylight. Right?"

"Yes, Uncle Theo."

"Skin's getting yellower. Any sores?"

"No."

"But you can tell it's more yellow."

"I can tell."

"Growing any hair yet?"

She does not answer and he limps into the room.

"I said, are you growing any hair yet?" The voice is strident, angry. "You going to tell me or do I have to look?"

"No, no, Uncle Theo. There's hardly any. Anywhere. Really. Maybe a little fuzz here and there." She shrinks farther into herself on the rocker, legs tucked.

"All right." Father Theo turns toward the window and Rich ducks out of sight. Nearing his parked truck he stops, the gagging sensation overpowering, and retches. He had seen Father Theo's face clearly for the first time, without hat, upturned collar, or subterfuge.

It is not only ambivalence that keeps Rich Johnson away the next few days, that mixture of morbid fascination and repugnance of something awful which he cannot fathom, which he wonders at times if he is imagining. Dollars and cents and greed keep him occupied. The wolf pack has definitely moved back into the area and the opportunity, unpredictable and random, must be seized. He determines which runways are active, where the pack tends to move, and proceeds with his arrangements. He is too busy to spy on the occupants of Werewolf House.

Rich does not really believe they would turn into wolves, but experiences occasional flashes of suspicion and fear. He remembers the fluorescing teeth, the hairy priest, and feels his own insides roil. He says "poppycock" aloud to distract himself and goes on with his work.

The moon is nearly full, the pit in the woods is dug to a depth of over six feet with steep, sheer sides. The remains of the calving of the past week, when two cows had given birth, had been stored in green plastic sacks to ripen and are now in the bottom of the pit. The sacks, turned inside out, have been dragged around the rim of the pit area to distribute the scent.

It's been baited two days, he says to himself, time to check it out. Surefooted in the moonlight, Rich Johnson makes his way through the woods. There is a wolf howl in the distance, and answering howls, and the man grimaces in annoyance. If the pack is out howling it will be far from the pit. But nearing it, he hears slight movement and approaches carefully, peering down lest it contain a skunk or some other wildlife. Three timber wolves are at the bottom. Three!

"Bastards!" he hisses, throwing his hat at them. "God, how I hate you goddamned critters!" He tears off his jacket and throws it into the pit. "Smell that!"

The wolves shrink from the clothing but have little room to retreat. Rich pulls the hunting knife from its sheath at his hip and leaps in.

The wolves flatten to the ground and roll over in submission, lips pulled back in the rictus of surrender. It is the same fawning, grovelling as is displayed by the lesser, weaker ones within the pack as alpha asserts his position.

With swift movements the woodsman cuts the leg tendons, then hoists the first animal to the top. "Run if you can, you son of a bitch," Rick pants. "I'll be up there to finish you off in a while."

He disables and removes the second, breathing harder from exertion, and turns to the third. This animal squirms and writhes, but he cuts the tendons quickly. Rich sheathes the knife and rises to sling the wolf topside when he sees his visitors.

Father Theo and the girl Lisa are standing at the rim watching him. They are plain and clear in the moonlight, large eyes fixed on him, their sallow skin almost white. Both are grimacing and their teeth glow red.

"God Almighty!" Rich faints.

"There's no doubt they saw you?" Ben asks. They are standing by the gas pump next afternoon.

"Plain. Took one of the wolves. Left the other one and the one in the pit."

"You asshole! If they tell anybody . . . "

"Who're they to tell anybody anything? Goddamn werewolves. Should kill 'em, Ben, like they was plain wolves. Fucking witches is what they are, weirdos."

"They hurt you any?"

"No."

"Didn't suck your blood or nothing? No teeth marks on your neck?" Ben is grinning, his beer paunch pressing against the lanky woodsman's middle, the fat index finger poking Rich Johnson's chest. "I don't know about you, Rich. D'you drink any last night?"

"No, I wasn't drinking, you know better. And I wasn't careless neither."

"Fancy imagination you got," Ben shakes his head. "Never took you t'go for kiddie stories. Werewolves!"

"I'm not makin' it up, Ben. It's true. I'll show you!"

"You bring the pelts? Get rid of the carcasses, the pit?"

"No, Ben. Sorry. Had all I could do just to make it here."

"You sure a sad case, Rich. I'll finish inside and then we'd better get 'em 'n clean up the pit. An' do something about your friends out there. Werewolves! A sick priest and a scrawny kid, werewolves." Ben shakes his head. "You eat anything? No? Come in grab a bowl a chili while I change an' we'll go. You crazy careless son of a bitch. Come on, Rich."

It is moonlight when they approach the house on foot. They hear the nearby howl and the distant responses. Rich, in the lead, freezes, jabs his elbow into Ben's midriff, and Ben nods. Closer now they hear Father Theo's highpitched, rasping voice behind the house.

Lupus! Lupus!

Versipellis

Moving alongside the house, craning around the corner, they watch Father Theo chant, screech, gesticulate, beseeching the moon. He is naked, his body covered by patches of long gray hair. He crawls on all fours, rises hunched and bent-shouldered to gesticulate; he alternately howls and chants. Finally he sits on the ground in abject surrender, a cowering beta.

"Nothing works," he whispers. "It's all useless." As he turns his head they see the lips drawn back in a snarl, and the teeth glow red in the moonlight.

"Mother of God!" Ben utters, his hand a tightening vise on the woodsman's arm. They tense, ready to flee as the naked figure slowly rises and makes its way to the back door and goes in.

Rich tugs at Ben's jacket to follow. They scurry to the front window and watch Father Theo drag himself into the candlelit room. The girl is nowhere to be seen but the man seems to be talking to her, or at her, if not to himself, and they hear snatches of his monologue.

" . . . a curse on our family. Your mother had it. D'you hear? She died from it. Hear me?"

They hear no answer from the child.

" . . . done every rite of exorcism from the church but the evil only gets worse. I found ancient Latin and Greek rituals in the archives but they're useless. Useless!"

He totters about, collapses at the table, head on his arms, rouses again.

"Come here, girl. I said come here!" He staggers out of sight and they hear drawers opening and closing. "Come in here. Now!"

"She's getting worse," he mutters. "A lot worse. Poor cursed thing. Lisa, it doesn't matter if you aren't dressed. Come in here in your shift."

They still cannot see the girl but he crosses their view. He is still naked, a furry, misshapen figure with sores, a length of wire stretched between his hands.

"Say your prayers," they hear him order her.

"I'm chilly, Uncle Theo. I'm scared."

"Pray."

There is an indistinct mumble, his voice intermixed with hers.

"What the hell's going on?" Ben whispers.

Rich shrugs, uses his knife to pry the window up a fraction.

" . . . never grow into a woman, have children, lead a normal life. None of the good things, the joys . . . "

"Don't! Uncle Theo you're hurting me! Get off me!"

Thumping, thrashing, scrabbling from inside, then:

"Help! Aaaaarrghhh . . . "

Drumming on the wood floor and silence.

Ben straightens. For all his bulk he moves with fluidity and speed. He bursts through the door, raises the baseball bat he has been carrying, and the thwacking crack sounds like a shot to Rich who is still outside the window. He too rushes into the house and sees the body of Father Theo lying across that of the child, the back of the priest's skull smashed and oozing blood and brains.

The two men look at each other. Ben tosses the bat into the room, goes outside and returns with an armload of split firewood. Rich helps him. Silently they pile the wood about the room, find the kerosene can and douse the piles, making a trail out the door. They strike a match to the end of the trail and leave.

Doc Brandt and Clem Stanley are drinking coffee at Fishbone, their clothes smeared with soot and dirt. Rich and Ben are sitting with them but the silence hangs.

"Too bad about your Aunt Emma's old place," Rich finally says, "and them people burning up."

Doc continues to stare into his coffee cup, then looks up at the sheriff's man who nods slightly.

"Place didn't belong to me any more," Doc says. "I'm here as County Medical Examiner. Now, I'll tell you what I found. Then I want some questions answered. You two answer them and maybe that'll be all there's to it. If you don't I'll order an inquest and there's likely to be a grand jury right behind it."

"What's the uproar, Doc? Just a couple people died in a accident, wood stove or somethin'?" Rich whines and Ben kicks him under the table too late.

"I'll tell you," Doc snaps. "That fire was set, there are kerosene traces in the wood that didn't burn. Several places in that house. The priest's skull was smashed . . ."

"Maybe they spilled some kerosene," Rich says. "T'start the fire. And a beam fell on the man. Maybe they wanted t'kill theirselves, who knows."

"Shut up," Doc barks.

"Shut up," Ben yells at the same instant and Clem looks away.

"You'll get your chance to talk." Doc is angry, "And you'll do plenty of it. Right now you listen. We know he was killed before the fire. And we know the fire was set. You can argue if you want, but we have the physical proof. And you'll also have to explain how the girl was garrotted and the wire still around her neck."

"What's garrotted?" Rich asks.

"Like choked," Ben says. "Now shut up."

"And I've got reason to believe she was raped," Doc says. "Did you animals do that? Rape a child? Did you?"

"No, no," Rich pleads, "I wouldn't do nothin' like that."

"The hell you wouldn't." Doc glares at Rich. "Word is you do your own kin, brag about breaking in your own daughters, tying them to the bed. If what I suspect is true, and I'll know in a couple of days when I get the lab reports, I'll see you brought to trial and locked up the rest of your life!"

"I swear t'God, Doc, nothin' like that happened!" Rich is frantic. "They was crazy. They was werewolves!"

"What the hell is this, the Middle Ages? Burning witches? People move here and maybe get in the way of your poaching you have to kill them?" Doc is furious, his face mottled with anger spots.

"They really was werewolves, Doc, you got to believe me," Rich begs. "I'll tell ya, honest to God, everything!"

Ben leans back in his chair, his shoulders slumping, and they unfold the story, telling it all except for the pit trap and the killing of the wolves.

"Superstitious ignorant fools," Doc mutters when the two men are done. They call Indians savages, he thinks, yet Indians take in the sick and disabled and show them pity, acceptance, and care.

"Not just you two. The priest, too. Haven't you people ever heard of porphyria? I suppose not. What a price we pay for ignorance and a lack of respect. All the suffering and harm." He shakes his head and stares out the window but sees nothing of the woods.

"They weren't werewolves or anything supernatural," he finally says. "They had porphyria."

"What's that? Can you catch it, like if they bite? Or ya touch 'em?"

"It's genetic. Inherited. Rare now, but in some forms it gives people that yellow color and the sores, and hair patches."

"How come he howled and had fangs and all?"

"They become disfigured from the pain. That's what makes their lips draw back. He didn't have fangs, just normal teeth. With his lips drawn back they showed more."

"But I seen them glow in the dark. We both seen them. And they glowed red. I mean t'tell ya, red!" Rich's voice is near hysteria.

"Of course they glowed. The teeth fluoresce and in the moonlight they fluoresce red. Porphyria results in the body being unable to absorb iron and . . . look, it's complicated, but science understands it. And we can treat it if we find out about it."

"Whatcha gonna do, Doc?" Ben is still worried. "Goin' ta report everything?"

"I'll let you know, or Clem will. Meanwhile stay away from the place."

"What are you going to do?" Clem asks as they drive back. "They didn't harm the girl. They did kill the priest and torch the place, but they could claim they were trying to save the girl. Serve anybody or anything to make a case?"

Doc stares out the car window, watching the trees flit past, his thoughts far away. It pains him that whites are so unnatural, so tuned out of any balance with nature that they consider it normal to massacre wildlife and the land, turn their backs on those sick and ailing and helpless. Wanton. So wanton. Is it so hard to see yourself as part of the whole, as equal in creation with others? With plants and living things?

"What?" Doc turns to Clem. "Didn't hear you."

"I was saying I never heard of this porphyria either."

"Not surprising," Doc answers. "Very rare now. We think most of the carriers were wiped out during the Plague and then the witch hunts, when they burned as witches anybody who was different. More common in ancient times. Greeks and Romans had wolf cults; scared of them. Middle Ages too. With a lot of inbreeding they had places it was prevalent."

Not in America, Doc thinks. Somehow it didn't get here. And to Indians wolves were part of the natural order, and in the old teachings and legends occupied a very special place as man's helper, Nanabozho's brother who taught him to hunt and survive. Until the evil swallowed up Wolf Brother after he had fallen through the ice and into the depths where the evil lurked. Then Nanabozho took revenge.

Is that what I am supposed to do, wreak vengeance, Doc muses? But I'm not Nanabozho; I am Loon Dodaim, the healers, the peacemakers. Then how do you heal, make peace with the destructive ones like Ben and Rich? Doc feels the distaste rising in him like bile. He doesn't know.

"Never met or saw either of them," Doc says. "I'm not saying I would have spotted it if I had seen them. Maybe. I don't know."

After a while Doc says, "I suppose he was intending to kill himself after he strangled the girl. They become insane in those last stages. Not just from pain. Some biochemical thing. Poor, pitiful creatures."

Clem asks, "What are you going to do?" When Doc doesn't answer, Clem repeats, "What's to be done?"

Doc rolls down the window of the moving car and tosses out the laboratory samples. "Accidental death from fire," he says. "Take more than the two of us to change superstition and stupidity." And evil, he thinks.

DROPOUT

That bright 11th grader's dropped out." Frank Walters was disdainful. He taught chemistry, physics, and math in the small town high school. A meticulous, demanding man, overpowering to most students at six foot six with a saturnine face and stentorian voice, he pretended a take-it-or-leave-it attitude toward them. In fact he stayed after school for hours working with promising youngsters, prodding, challenging. "Can't prove the principle? Try the experiment again, bring me the formula when you have it." Again and again, until the student solved the problem without shortcut help.

"Which bright youngster?" Jacobi, English and social studies, was as short as the other was tall, an equally dedicated teacher.

"There's only one bright one in this year's junior class," Walters snapped. "Whyn't you go find him and talk to him? He's a potential for Harvard, Yale, Princeton, whatever. Now he's quit school. Gone three weeks."

It had to be Chubbles. "Why me?" Jacobi was not going to make it easy for Walters. They were good friends, sparring partners in the hallways, shouting mock insults at one another, going to social gatherings, concerts and plays together. Both were strict disciplinarians who rarely had to exercise discipline. Jacobi knew why Walters wanted him to find the boy, but he wanted to hear him say it.

"Because you're both Indian." Walters knew he'd been had, spun away and strode off.

Students referred to the two behind their backs as Mutt and Jeff. They also nicknamed Walters "Dracula", and Jacobi "Fearless Fosdick" because he would go anywhere, confront anyone if it meant helping a student in difficulties. When a pregnant girl dropped out of school, Jacobi went to the home to arrange tutoring, childcare after the birth, and talked her back into school despite her parents' shamed refusal to cooperate. When a group of high school athletes cornered the girl at her locker and teased her cruelly, she took her books to the school office and left for good. Not even Jacobi could talk her back.

He found out who the ringleaders were, lectured the entire class for two hours, then made a home visit to the principal offender telling the parents, "Your boy has done something really sick and needs help. Counseling or something. I want to talk to him alone." And Jacobi did, succinctly and at length. That one of the parents was on the school board and a middle class government employee at the Bureau of Indian Affairs was irrelevant.

"Life doesn't tolerate malicious, gratuitous cruelty," Jacobi told the boy face to face in the family's basement rec room. "What you did, and got others to join in doing, did irreparable harm to the life of that girl. She had done none of you any harm. She was a fat, homely child abused at home and raped by her uncle. She was a helpless victim and you victimized her some more. She will never return to school, will never get the education that was her one chance to get out of her miserable life. All the "I'm-sorries" won't fix that. You have a responsibility to fix the evil in you. Find out why you did it, what made you do this. It's up to you and your parents to get you counseling. Your conscience will be watching."

Now Jacobi set out to track the missing scholar.

"Haven't seen him." "Hasn't been hanging out." "Dunno." Schoolmates were no help. Chubbles was moderately popular, a fat kid in elementary school, still short and chubby in high school and a non-athlete. He was brighter, quicker than the rest, offsetting this handicap with an ingratiating personality, a ready smile and an endless repertory of jokes. His mouse-brown hair and relatively light complexion facilitated constrained acceptance among Indians and whites.

Chubbles Rasmussen's home was a travesty. The single-story frame had once, long ago, sheltered an unsuccessful small holding farmer on a stolen Indian allotment. No one, neither government nor tribe, had ever made an effort to get the property back in Indian hands, and Leona Rasmussen rented it from the absentee white owners. No discernible work had been done to maintain, much less improve, the ramshackle house. Trash, debris, car parts and car bodies surrounded the place, a little Tobacco Road amid the pine forest. It was the place that rednecks and supercilious whites pointed to as typical Indian life-style and housing, even though it was an exception, the only such on the whole tract. All Rasmussens lived there when they were not off drunk, sleeping in a car or on someone's floor, or in jail. Leona, once pretty and now blowsy, had seven sons and daughters, one of whom was as pretty as her mother had once been. Chubbles was the youngest of the lot, a neat and tidy anachronism amid the dishevelment. People joked that the seven young Rasmussens had at least 70 fathers. Leona still had a steady parade of boyfriends.

"Come in . . . close door it's cold . . . Oh, it's Jacobi . . . come on sing with us." A babble of slurred voices, a stench of stale beer.

Eyes glazed, Leona was sprawled on a ragged, filthy couch. Her hair was matted and stringy, her face had a patina of grime. She did not acknowledge Jacobi.

"C'mon, Jacobi, have a beer," someone pressed.

"He can't, he's alcoholic, been straight forever," another said. "I'm not alcoholic, I drink."

"So what's he want here?" Bellicose. One of the eight or nine men sitting on the floor amid beer cans.

The house should have been cold, encased as it was in shrunken clapboard and insulated with wood shavings long since compacted at the bottom of the walls, faced by buffalo board with holes punched in fights. A barrel stove overheated the place; trails of wood chips led from the door to the stove.

They all looked at Jacobi.

"I'm looking for Chubbles."

"Ain't here."

"Seen him? The last few days?"

No one had. Discussion about who had last seen Chubbles turned acrimonious and led to a near fight.

"He was here just a while ago!"

"Wasn't either, that was last party!"

"Goddamn stuck-up kid, one time he drinks up all the beer, next time he's too stuck-up t'be seen with us!"

"Whatcha want with him anyhow?" one of the older brothers asked. "Hasn't been in school in two weeks."

"Schoolboy's quit, hunh? Well, he ain't been here in a while. Here, we'll sing for ya." The brother picked up a battered dishpan, dumped a loaded ashtray on the floor and used it to beat.

They had trouble getting the song going and Jacobi winced. It was supposed to be a powwow song, a prayer by dancing, a thanksgiving to the Creator for beautiful life and creation.

"Ah, shit, let's do the Air Force song. C'mon, Jacobi, you used ta sing, get us started."

"Not tonight, some other time," Jacobi parried. "Got to find the kid." He left, grieving over the maudlin desecration.

Spiritual life, traditional ceremonies, and songs were sacred to Jacobi. Sacred and very private. Not even his good friend Frank Walters had an inkling that Jacobi attended seasonal gatherings of the old religious society, made his daily tobacco offerings, fasted once a year, or entered the sweat lodge. Jacobi felt, knew, that Walters would neither understand nor accept. A line had been drawn in the sand of their relationship.

He found Chubbles at the coffeeshop hangout two blocks from the school the next afternoon, telling jokes to classmates.

"Let's go for a ride." Jacobi leaned over the back of the booth. "I have something to show you." It was an offer the boy could not refuse, surrounded as he was by his peers. It was not the time nor place for a confrontation, and he did not feel like arguing. Besides, his curiosity was piqued.

Jacobi drove nine miles out of town, across the bridge, and parked on the shoulder of the road. On both sides were wild rice fields, the winding river fanning into lakes. A world of beige marshes and blue lakes backed by dark green forests stretched for miles either way. Upstream the river banks rose amid higher ground.

"What's out here?" The boy was nervous.

Short, stocky Jacobi waved both arms expansively. "Eagle nest over there. Had two fledglings this year. Ancient place, this. Used to be rice camps, storage pits long ago. On the shore this other way. Back in those trees, sugar bush. Come."

He led. The chubby boy, a little shorter, followed across a ditch, up over an embankment, down to the riverbank. Jacobi walked along the water's edge, sidestepping occasional wavelets, hunched, peering down. Suddenly he stopped and sat down on the grassy bank. He beckoned Chubbles to follow and sit next to him.

"Know what this place is?"

Chubbles shook his head no.

"Look around. Figure it out."

The boy looked in all directions and finally shook his head.

"Look in the water. D'you see anything?"

"The river, rocks."

"What kind of rocks?"

"Big ones. Boulders. Under the water. Like, in a row . . . " the boy hesitated.

Jacobi let it hang there. Finally he said, "If they're in a row, like stepping stones or a bridge, where would they lead?"

"To the other side." Chubbles grinned.

"And what's over there? If you keep going?"

Chubbles thought. "Sugar bush, then Toad Lake and the rice beds."

Jacobi nodded. "This is an old stone bridge. Prehistoric. Water level was lower then, the dam downstream has raised it. Used as a shortcut to get over there, also for spearing fish coming through the opening in the middle. See, the bridge is V-shaped. Also helped to back up water so canoes could get through during low water in the summer; there was a little riffle, rapids, down there."

"How old is it?"

The teacher looked out over the water. "Maybe two thousand. Maybe more. They found remnants of a fishing village 5,000 years old downstream during road construction."

Chubbles looked up and down the river. "That's a long time."

"Our ancestors have been here a long time. A very long time. Much of our land's been taken, our religion ridiculed and almost destroyed. Traditions forbidden and a lot of them lost. Forgotten. That's why we need you, others like you, to become leaders, save what's left, bring back what you can."

They sat in silence gazing at the water, the backdrop forest.

"How'd you learn all this stuff?"

Jacobi thought a while. "I had an elder. I brought him tobacco to teach me. He accepted it." It sounded casual, diffident, but it wasn't at all. Jacobi made it as a serious one-time offer. In the old ways one did not proselytize. Individuals were expected to know about these matters from family and the community. It went against the beliefs to exhort and urge someone to make a personal commitment entailing work and dedication and an ethical way of life. If the boy brought him tobacco he would accept it and would begin the long instruction. Take him into the sweat lodge, teach him about the sacred scrolls, the responsibilities, the pipe, making a sacred fire, the ceremonies, the complex matrix of traditional Indianness. He prayed the boy would respond, if not immediately, at some time.

"You can do that too. Bring tobacco. You're needed," Jacobi finally said. "Your gifts are needed by the people. There are very few individuals who can succeed in both worlds. Come back to school to get an education."

It took a while. Finally Chubbles nodded.

"Tomorrow?"

Chubbles nodded again.

Walters and Jacobi prodded, wrote letters, obtained scholarships, campaigned with the other teachers and administrators, some of whom disdained Indians. Chubbles was the first high school graduate to be admitted to an Ivy League college. He came back to visit after his freshman year, Joe College in person, not quite so chubby, bubbling. Two years passed before he reappeared, seen around town with his older brothers, looking and acting like them. Word was he had quit college, tired of the grind. Chubbles was anchored to the two ends of his life's yo-yo, the vision of what he could be at one end, at the other the terrible draw of self-destruction learned at his mother's breast and cemented by his family ties, his niveau.

At the end of a school day Jacobi was making his weary way to his car and found Chubbles leaning against the vehicle.

"Guess you heard." The young man had put on weight again and looked the worse for wear. Jacobi took it all in and nodded.

"Couldn't take it any more," Chubbles explained. "Too much pressure." Jacobi waited, saying nothing.

"But I'm going back in the fall. Aren't you going to take me to the river? Give me a lecture? Ask me to walk on water like Jesus?" There was a sarcastic edge to Chub's voice, a defensiveness masking shame, a harbinger of a personality trait which, if unchecked, could become vitriolic.

Jacobi shook his head. "Buy you a cup of coffee."

"You haven't said anything," Chubbles said over their empty pie plates, fingering a refilled coffee cup.

They had talked reservation politics and personalities, the housing program and rumors of economic development, skirting everything personal and the obvious.

"What's your plan when you've finished college?" Jacobi finally asked. "Grad school?"

Chubbles, solemn until then, grinned. "Harvard. Business administration. An MBA. I've been accepted, I just needed a little vacation, a break from the pressures and conforming. Had to get back home and live a real life for a while. They were anxious for Indian students, makes them look good, gives them something to brag about. Full scholarship, allowance, the works. I got all the traffic would bear without even raising a sweat."

Jacobi managed a half-smile. "You can handle it. I know you can. I'll be retiring next year. Let me know how it goes. And . . ."

Chubbles waited. "And . . ?"

Jacobi wanted to say something about bringing tobacco, about setting the deep spiritual roots that help a human being walk a straight course. There were many kinds of successes, but only one Red Road. This boy, this brilliant product of devastation could be one of those rare comets that illuminated and inspired, led others back to the Red Road in the new, changing society. But he had made the offer once, told him about bringing tobacco once, and now the choice was with Chubbles. He should not say it again; the old teachings were based on a novitiate's choice, not on proselytizing. Chubbles had come part of the way, but his hands were still empty of tobacco, his heart still scattered like spilled mercury.

"And . . . good luck."

Twice more Chubbles came to see Jacobi with years interspersed and no communication in between. Each time the aging, retired teacher involuntarily glanced at his visitor's hands to see if one perhaps held tobacco. The first time Jacobi was finishing a hand drum. The hide had not tightened properly. He had had to wet and stretch it and was just tying off when an unfamiliar car drove into the yard. He put away the drum and walked out to greet his visitor. It was unusual for Jacobi to have drop-in company; he was a very private, almost secretive person. Students saw the public persona, the demanding and caring teacher. A few friends, such as Walters, saw an educated, sophisticated and knowledgable man with a puckish sense of humor. But Jacobi, long a childless widower, kept the facets of his being separate. Perhaps only a few intimates among the older Indians with whom he shared traditional spiritual life and practices had a full sense of Jacobi's being.

He paused momentarily before he recognized Chubbles.

"My, haven't you changed!"

Chubbles had lost weight and gained confidence. He smiled at the compliment, a self-assured, pleased smile; apparently he no longer needed to ingratiate himself.

"Come in, come in." Jacobi led the way into his kitchen and set out coffee cups. "I saw in the papers you finished Harvard cum laude. Congratulations!"

It was Chubbles' first visit to Jacobi's home in the woods, a small and meticulously kept house. Most students, though they knew where he lived, would not have dared intrude.

"You're surely besieged by corporate offers." Jacobi peered over the rim of his cup.

"There've been some. I interned summers. Chicago one year, with Malleable Steel. New York at Paine Webber. Worked part time in Boston last year."

Yes, the young man had panache. Jacobi nodded and waited.

Chubbles pulled a glistening tooled leather wallet from an inside pocket of his sports coat. He extracted a business card and handed it across the table.

"Emerson 'Chub' Rasmussen," Jacobi read. "Tribal Administrator and Business Manager, Mahng Lake Reservation." Chub had brought his old teacher a gift: "See, I have accomplished what you wanted for me; I have the education and the social skills to do great things for my people." Unspoken, it emanated through every pore.

Jacobi's face showed pleasure, but his heart plummeted: the promising young man had stepped into a minefield from which there might be no return. Surely, bright as he was, he must know of the perpetual fraud and corruption in the tribal government. It had been petty, small potato stuff in the past, no less evil that there was so little to share: padding expense accounts, going on needless boondoggle trips to gamble, drink and whore. Steering part-time, temporary jobs to relatives or supporters. The last few years all that had changed. Now it was big money.

The court victory reclaiming hunting and fishing rights netted the small reservation several hundred thousand dollars a year in state rebates from license fees. Federal grants for housing, health, and road construction increased the flow into the millions. Then the gambling craze caught up and the reservation built casinos which did a land-office business. The needs were there all right, for housing, health, roads. The hunting fees and gambling profits could buy the infra-structure: the community centers, the economic development, the scholarships to train the young. All the ingredients were there, but none of it had happened. Yet. And no public accounting of any of the monies had ever been made. Meanwhile tribal officials bought elec-tions, stuffing ballot boxes with fictitious absentee ballots and voting the graveyards to reassure a return to office. Jobs, benefits, houses went to supporters. Tribal attorneys and satraps frequented restau-rants and bars, pulling thousand-dollar bills from coat pockets. The pitiful conditions in which the people had found themselves before the avalanche of money remained the same.

Would the brilliant Chub be strong enough to withstand this ocean, this ebb and tide of evil? Would a young man emerging from a boyhood of alcoholism, fatherlessness, spiritual suicide have the character, the skills, to bring about change? Jacobi knew on the instant that he could facilitate Chub's education, but could not influence the spiritual gyroscope—not unless it was sought, unless tobacco was offered, which Jacobi would take. Gladly! But it had as yet to come. "It will be difficult to be a straight arrow," Jacobi said.

"I can handle it." Chub was confident.

"For 150 years the government staffed the Indian Bureau with the most corrupt and incompetent employees and put cashiered army officers in the Civil Service." Jacobi stared at his hands enfolding the coffee cup. "The misfits and political debts they didn't know what to do with. We were taught by them. Those were the role models, the instructors. At the same time our tribal structures, our social and political checks and balances, our moral system, were systematically destroyed. So I'm not harsh about our tribal politics today, I understand it. But it's time for something better." He looked up at the young man, the message clear. "It'll be difficult. Lonely. You'll need strength. You have the education, the intelligence. Now you'll need that something extra."

"I can handle it." A young man's confidence? Sense of invincibility? Hubris?

At sunset that evening Jacobi, alone again, made a small ceremonial fire at the rock where he offered his customary prayers. He made his offerings and sat at the fire long after it had burned out, long after the evening star heralded the advent of the nighttime canopy, long after full dark had fallen, illuminated by those stars of the universe visible to the human eye, impervious to the gathering chill.

Over a very few years, three or four at most, Chub carved a meteoric career as tribal administrator. He came to sit on the boards of directors of various national Indian organizations, was written about in magazines and newspapers. His personal appearance metamorphosed accordingly: his skin was darkened, giving him a more Indian appearance, but it was never so dark as to worry the whites with whom he dealt; his hair was tinted subtly darker, masking the non-Indian lightness. He often dressed in blue blazer and gray slacks, always white shirts and becoming neckties. Immaculately turned out at all times, he had slimmed down and kept his weight stable.

Chub was said to be obtaining more housing funds, negotiating the move of a factory from the Cities to the rez, a polished, busy man of the times. Jacobi heard about it even though they did not visit. Chub didn't run the casinos which were expanding and burgeoning now with an ancillary motel, now with a nearby liquor store—Chub ran the people who ran the casino. He had become a power to be reckoned with. Then a low murmur, an undercurrent, was whispered, alluded to indirectly in private conversations.

People told of incidents when Chub was brusque, impatient, arrogant. He had a mean streak, accusing those who differed with him of outrageous, baseless sins. He said an elderly tribal officer who rejected a contested land request from one of Chub's brothers was in the pay of the other party, a blatant lie, but it besmirched the old man who resigned in the face of the rumors. Chub didn't do it often, but the few outbursts came to characterize him among the poor and disfranchised as a tool of the "ins" and opposed to the peoples' interests.

Chub arrived at Jacobi's on a Saturday midmorning, dressed for once in a checked flannel shirt which looked brand new, and creased slacks. The outfit had a prissy, make-believe look that said, "Look at me, I'm just plain folks!" Jacobi had been working in the yard, his dented pickup truck loaded with rocks and split firewood. Chub did not realize his old mentor was gathering supplies for a sweat that night.

"Come in, you're just in time."

"In time for what?"

"Coffee time."

Chub was fidgety. "Hate to tell you this," he finally blurted, "but I can't do it. The straight arrow stuff. I have my relations to take care of." Unspoken was Chub's secret dream, building a nest egg large enough to finance personal independence and public acceptance, eventually sufficient recognition to propel him to the University Board of Regents, to a Presidential appointment. Commissioner of Indian Affairs? A cabinet post? Secretary of Interior? He sat at the table, uncomfortable, not knowing what else to say.

"They need decent houses, jobs," Chub offered after a while. "I had to use my position to get the land, the houses. Mom's getting along in years." Unsaid: the land was allotments stolen from Indian owners long ago that rightly should have gone to the heirs, not the tribal official's relations.

"You have enough money to buy each of them a house," Jacobi said acidly, knowing that the mother, Leona, had been in and out of detox and the hospital countless times, that a sister was following the mother not only in looks but also in life-style, that brothers had been in increasingly serious trouble—lately for armed robbery and assault with intent to kill. "That housing money is supposed to help the poor and the elderly. That's a perversion. And you're just enabling your folks to go on drinking, instead of telling them you'll help once they straighten out."

Chub's head was down, he sat mute.

"What is this, some form of embezzled heaven? A distorted Christianity? Do good deeds, knowing they're wasted, so you'll get a halo and wings in the hereafter?" Jacobi was fuming.

It was more than that and both knew it. Blood thicker than water, my family right or wrong, the whole tribal political aura of making hay while the sun shines, and the people be damned.

"I know what you wanted for me, from me," he said, getting up, anxious to leave. "I'm sorry." His coffee cup remained full, a bit of cream coagulating in the top skim.

Jacobi knew what would happen, he could sense it, even if he could not predict the particulars. At the sweat that night the aging man called for four doors, for many hot rocks, and he prayed and sang a long time. This helped, but when he emerged from the lodge he still felt sorrow.

Two very different auras fluttered around Chub in the months and years following. He sat on the Governor's Human Rights Commission, was honored by his alma mater, and assumed a persona in white and national Indian power circles. Among the people on the rez there was the other. He was the secret owner of the liquor store, working through a fronting dummy corporation; he formed a firm, again through a dummy corporation together with his brothers whose names he used, to lease slot machines to the tribal casinos and to furnish the bingo supplies, that endless stream of paper forms for which there was perpetual demand; he bought land, turned around and sold it to the tribe at an astronomical profit. He had insider information, sitting in on the decision to purchase the property. People suspected but they did not know, there was no proof. There was still no public accounting of all the funds coming in and going out. Here and there people complained, a few wrote letters to state and federal officials, and twice there were rag-tag pickets waving protest posters in front of the tribal headquarters. But nothing happened and no government officials seemed to care. The incumbents or their look-alikes kept getting reelected, voting procedures and ballot box tampering immune from both state and federal control. Hidden behind the elected officials and immune from it all was Chub.

The balloon burst came when the status quo of corruption seemed inviolate. A Federal Grand Jury voted a bill of indictments against Chub and others for fraud running into the millions of dollars. Now it was public knowledge that they had secretly formed a phantom corporation which owned the slot machines which they leased to the reservation's casinos and had a monopoly on the casino's bingo supplies. It was discovered by federal auditors who stumbled across a suspicious invoice, then another, the trail eventually leading to Chub. The trail went back many years. First they had skimmed some tribal funds and invested them in a liquor store, then a small chain of such stores, for which a non-Indian fronted. With the profits they invested in, and ultimately took control of the two corporations. The money trails were convoluted and eventually some, but not all, were traced by the government investigators.

Paradoxically, many Indians hooted and cheered while middle and upper class whites, the power brokers in the larger community, were disbelieving and incredulous, and some of them accused the government prosecutors of racial prejudice and persecution. To these whites Chub had been, finally, a "good" Indian, a man to whom they could relate, who spoke their language.

All that talk died quickly during the trial as the evidence, painstakingly and quietly accumulated over many months, was presented. Chub was convicted but the sentencing delayed, delayed again and again. People were puzzled but attorneys understood. The prosecutors were sweating Chub: give us the evidence, the proof we need to prosecute and convict the others in on the schemes, and you walk with a slap on the wrist. Fail to give it, and you put in hard time, lots of it, in a federal prison.

In the world at large it wouldn't matter which path Chub chose. He was ruined, his reputation and career permanently compromised. Whether he saved his own skin from prison and delivered his co-conspirators to the authorities, or whether he took the prison time, mattered only to them. For Chub it was lose-lose; he had sidestepped the straight road, the Red Road, and taken the wrong fork long ago.

In the end he tried a finesse which worked, sort of. He carefully coached the others, advised what records to destroy, whose silence to buy, and delivered to the prosecutors the useless leftovers. None of them went to prison, and each lapsed into obscurity. Jacobi followed all this only peripherally. He did not need to know the details; he already knew the gist of it and felt the pain.

"Maybe it was my fault in part," the old teacher said at his prayer rock. "How could he know about bringing tobacco if no one ever explained why you did it? I failed to do that; I only told him to bring it. I should have reached out more; he had nothing in his home, his life, to give him a hint of how to live. You know, Grandfathers, he did come to me and told me he could not walk the straight path. If you guide him my way again, he still has his gifts, I will try to help, to teach. He has so many gifts, he really could help the people in many ways. Maybe he has learned from all this, maybe he has shed his false pride. Please send him back to me. Oh, and Grandfathers, if you send me another young person, I will teach and share my knowledge, not only of this world now, but also of the old ways. I won't expect them to know it. Thank you."

FELICE

If looks could kill the social worker would have dropped in the doorway. Felice felt poison and snapped her eyes but he just stood there, a blond man with a red face, with chest and shoulders of a wrestler or a football player. Felice knew why he was there and didn't help him a bit. She didn't say come in, sit down, what do you want, she just looked hate.

"I'm John Landgraf, from Social Services." He came in a few steps without an invitation. "Public Health doctor asked me to look in on her. Is she sick?" He knew the words were stupid, regretted them as they were uttered, but sight of the dark-skinned elfin woman with long, curling black hair distracted him.

"She's all right." Felice compounded the stupidity.

He noticed the piles of books, paperbacks and library books crammed into wooden orange crate shelves and stacked here and there. He remembered hearing about her, the bright and beautiful girl who was the despair of teachers who could not talk her into going on to college, the fey intellect who sensed that she would face perpetual alienation away from the reservation. A stranger in a foreign land whose language she did not want to learn. Rosalie's granddaughter. Even Rosalie had wanted it for her, but Felice had ignored that too saying, "You need me Grandma," but meaning I need you.

Landgraf noticed the flies in the tiny house settling on the old woman who brushed at them in birdwing movements.

"Wouldn't she be better off in a nursing home?" he asked.

101

"She's lived here most her life and wants to die here," Felice bit at him, "and I'll take care of her!" The look on her face, the rage within, said, "You rotten white son of a bitch like the rest of them. Put her in a nursing home, let her die among strangers ignoring her. Cardboardman! Chimokoman!"

"Doctor's worried about her taking medication regularly," Landgraf stumbled on, trying to do his job, trying to ignore the impact Felice had on him.

"Who is that man?" Rosalie croaked from her bed.

"Social worker nosying around, it's OK, Grandma."

"What's the matter with you girl invite him in, offer some coffee gotta be hospitable come on you know what's right if you don't I'll have to get up do it here I'll get the coffee . . . "

The old woman, small at the best of times but wizened now, slid her bony legs out from under the covers revealing rumpled nylons to the knees covered by heavy wool socks ankle high.

Felice noticed Landgraf's startled look and said, "She's always worn wool socks, winter and summer. Cold feet. Here, Grandma, I'll get the coffee, you get back to bed."

"Oh, I'm up now gotta be hospitable to company even if they is welfare you got commodities you ain't well all right sit down we'll get by." Rosalie's run-on speech required practice to decipher.

He came by a few days later and patched holes in the screen, a temporary favor because the sagging door and frame would stand only so much tinkering. This time he said nothing about Rosalie's medications and he knew better than to utter "nursing home."

Then he brought a rabbit he had shot because Felice had mentioned the old woman liked rabbit stew. Rosalie noticed his look of disappointment that Felice was not home, but he was too shy to ask and Rosalie too contrary to explain. Besides, what's to explain? The girl got tired of tending her and took off once in a while.

Rosalie turned to the wall, hiding a smile, and said, "Oh I really love rabbit that's nice waboose we call it you better start learning t'talk Indian you gonna see that girl come back soon I could get t'like you myself."

He kept coming back, making himself useful, trying not to make calf's eyes at Felice when she was there, trying not to ask about her whereabouts when she was not.

"Saw some partridge," Felice said one day. "Maybe if they sit still long enough you can hit one."

They drove to the boat landing and walked back on an overgrown logging trail to a stand of red pine so tall they shaded out all underbrush. The ground was cushioned in needles and duff. She stopped there and faced him and it was some moments before he realized that she wanted him. He was surprised and then the thinking was shoved aside in the embracing, the kissing, the lust.

"Do you use anything?" he asked.

She shook her head. "It's all right, come on!" Her lips were fuller, her color higher.

"Be right back." He loped down the trail.

She was sitting against a tree trunk, hair over her face and he could not read her expression. "You must be all worn out and tired from that walk," she said. "Better rest."

He picked her up then, threw her over his shoulder and whirled until both were dizzy and some of her long hair was plastered across his face and they found themselves standing face to face, and then making love abruptly, his hands holding her buttocks, her feet off the ground, and both quickly moving to completion. Later, more easily, they loved again.

They fit, they meshed, but there were also barriers that defied talking. In the days, weeks, months of the relationship she would disappear without explanation other than "I been to the store . . . to Old Peter's . . . " though she had been gone a day, two days, three.

Landgraf was baffled. He veered from jealousy to anger to dismay. Whenever he decided to break off the tantalizing relationship she would anticipate him and be forthcoming, even aggressive, and he was swept off his emotional feet again. Was she testing? Wanting to be sure? Punishing? She did not understand it any more than he.

Once he said, "Somebody said Dora, your mom, left you at Rosalie's when you were a kid and never came back. They . . . " Felice's mouth opened, froze in a grimace as though surgeons' retractors had pulled it apart and left a gaping wound from which no sound emerged. She plunged out of the house and did not come back for three days, lips puffy, love bruises on her neck.

There was no rhyme, reason, or explanation.

"Let's go to the Redwood and dance," she said.

He did not want that world of too-loud music blaring from the jukebox, the stink of stale smoke and staler beer. He did not want to deny her an evening out. He did not want her walking off in a huff, going there alone, going home with someone else? Coming back . . . when? "OK."

They sat with another couple, Felice's cousin David home from law school, as dark-skinned and raven-haired as Felice, but basketball player tall. David's date was a fellow student and both were up for the summer doing legal research for the reservation. David drank cokes all evening, but the others ordered pitchers of beer.

"Hey, slow down," Landgraf cautioned as Felice gulped glass after glass.

"Slow down yourself," she snapped, "you been keeping up with me. I know what I can handle."

"D'you want to dance?" he asked.

She looked at him disdainfully and shook her head.

A stranger came to ask and she went with him, a tall muscular young man in tight Levis that accentuated his crotch. The pair twisted and turned on the floor, hips, torsos moving in the mock ritual, the pseudo-sexual rite. Landgraf caught his breath watching Felice's body move . . . that way . . . with someone else. She never relaxed, opened up, dancing with him.

She brought the stranger to their table, hitched her chair closer pressing her side and leg against him. To Landgraf she said in an aside, "God, he's big, isn't he? Huge. D'you want to dance?" She was taunting, mocking him, and he was furious and shook his head.

"OK, if that's how you want it. You had your chance." There was a triumphant, victorious smile and she took the stranger to the floor.

The music tempo was slow and they danced close together, her arms around his neck, his around her waist and slipping lower, torsos rubbing against each other, then their feet no longer moved but they were glued at the crotch moving in dance-floor masturbation. She turned once to look at Landgraf, smiled, and turned back to her partner to hold him even tighter.

On the drive back to Rosalie's she said, "I'm glad we got out of there, he was really hustling me."

Landgraf stared at her, inchoate with fury: he was hustling you? He let her out vowing never to return, furious with her, with himself for not walking out, for not punching the stranger or Felice or both. He was back four days later.

One day when he stopped at Rosalie's as was becoming customary Felice had disappeared again, but Rosalie kept him hopping. "That tea is too weak and you put too much sugar in oh here's David and you got that girl with you tell her sit down too bring me that robe John." The high-pitched querulous voice ran on and on. "Where's that robe now I'm cold my feet feel like witches' tits so what's new in town don't tell me no I don't know where Felice went she come home and went to sleep and when I next looked she was gone didn't do a damn thing around here there that tea is better thank you John a Johnson boy brought over some venison cut off steaks John and fry 'em up there's potatoes somewhere too you all stay an' eat."

Landgraf found an old meat saw hanging in the shed and a dull butchering knife in the house. David's girlfriend, Ruth, helped him clear the table and watched in horrified fascination as Landgraf put the hind quarter on the table where it slithered and slipped as he tried to find purchase to hold it with one hand while waggling the saw around with the other. City-bred Ruth, buxom and blond, wanted to be helpful but didn't know how.

David was no help. He leaned back in his chair, tilting it on the rear legs, and laughed. Ruth struggled to hold the shank and Landgraf, now using both hands, wielded the two-foot-long saw. For once Rosalie was silent, watching with glittering eyes.

"Maybe if you made your cut with the knife," David suggested, "and used the saw just on the bone. Like that. No! Across the grain, across. Yeah, that's it." Hunger overcame fun.

"Goddamit, I've sawed into the goddamned table," Landgraf shouted.

Rosalie turned to the wall. Her body shook. David peered over her shoulder and saw tears on her cheeks. The old woman was wracked in paroxysms of laughter.

"Back in a minute," David muttered and walked out. Around the corner of the house he too bent over. Something told him he should go back and help, but he was laughing too hard to hear it.

"A car, there's a car!" Rosalie yelped. "The warden I bet it's the game warden if he smells this food if he comes in here you're all in a heap of trouble quick hide that meat no not what you're eating the rest of the hind quarter Christ God Almighty there's blood all over the table and the saw is out John for Christ's sake get a move on . . . "

The car did not stop. Landgraf sat in mesmerized paralysis fighting visions of arrest, publicity, jail, a fine, loss of his job.

"Wait a minute," Landgraf said. "It's legal for you to have venison this time of year. Isn't it?"

Rosalie and David nodded.

"Get me some more meat," Rosalie croaked. "And potatoes and dip some bread in that grease it's what we call punjigay yeah it's legal I'm just having fun you oughta come around more it's the best laugh I've had."

It was the last good belly laugh, too. The long-neglected gallbladder condition made it too painful and she was, after all, weakening. Too old and frail for surgery, too stubborn to watch her diet, Rosalie knew that even without the bothersome condition she would be, she was, approaching the door to the West.

"Move in stay with me," she said to Landgraf and he did, making do in the tiny shack, fixing her coffee and toast before leaving for work, preparing a fried dinner of sorts afterwards even though she ate sparingly and the morning toast was still there in the evening. Felice came and went, drinking beer with Landgraf until they staggered, collapsed into sleep. When she was gone, he drank by himself as the old woman's wakeful times became more sporadic and of shorter durations.

"Come back goddamit, I've had enough of your running out." Landgraf grabbed Felice's arm at roadside. He had chased after her as she walked stubbornly, unevenly along the pavement to town.

"Fuck off, leave me alone." She marched on to her syncopated drummer, torso rigid atop unsteady legs. "You meddling white son of a bitch redneck Okie bastard."

Landgraf left to return to Rosalie. Over his shoulder he saw a car make a bootlegger U-turn and stop beside Felice, who got in.

She'd been abandoned even before she was born. And again before she was a toddler. Twice. Two times before she could even speak she'd been told she wasn't good enough to love, to nurture. The man had left before Felice was born. He had left his job at the hardware store and transferred to another in the chain in another town, some said as an assistant manager or something, and had married a white woman there. A mystery figure shrouded in haze and withheld knowledge. The mother had come and gone, leaving the infant with one family or another saying she'd be back in a few hours, or tomorrow, until people got tired of it and complained to Social Services, who put her in foster homes. Then Dora got a job in the Cities, went on trips out West with a man, and did not come back at all. Dora had vanished altogether. Booze? Drugs? A pauper's grave? Buried in the desert? Nobody knew. Submerged, subsumed in the riptide of life.

Tiny, wizened, widowed Grandma Rosalie raised the girl, gave her shelter and caring, but it wasn't the same. The harm had been done, and all the extended family on the reservation, the countless cousins and playmates, weren't the same as an infant bonding with Mom or Dad, or Mom-and-Dad. The ur-bonding had never taken place, the need of it now encapsulated in a carapace. And now Rosalie's end was drawing near.

Over the weeks the once garrulous Rosalie became quiet, speaking with her eyes. One night Landgraf woke hearing rales. Some urge made him light the gentle kerosene lamp instead of pulling the cord on the overhead light. He sat on the edge of her cot, unsure whether to wake Felice, when the old woman grasped his hand. Hers was very cold. She held on tightly, her eye contact with him fading in and out, locking on him then disappearing into another world. Her raspy breathing became more uneven, the pauses between breaths longer, the resumptions shorter, until it all stopped and her eyes clouded and became rigid.

After the wake and the burial Felice disappeared and no one would tell him where she had gone, if indeed they knew. She was last seen on foot, walking the shoulder of the dirt road to the paved highway. Somebody, anybody, should have shouted help! Mayday! But there is no substitute for the inner voice, no surrogate weepers for the inner pain, and you can't hire a stand-in to fight your private wars.

A few weeks later Landgraf packed and left, his car loaded helter skelter and a twelve-pack by his side.

"Where am I? What place is this?"

A disembodied voice, a smell of disinfectant. "St. Mary's Hospital. Can you say your name?"

"F . . . f . . . Flice."

"Good. You'll be all right. Do you want something to drink? Eat?" Head shake and relapse into narcoleptic sleep.

Later. "Do you know where you are?"

"Ho . . . hos . . . hospital?"

"Good."

"How'd I get here?"

"You were found in a roadside ditch near the State Fairgrounds. St. Paul. Do you know what day it is? No? What year? In time, in time, it'll all make sense in time. Can you sit up? Good, here's a tray, try to eat what you can. You've been on IV nearly a week."

The gray murk lifted slowly. They made her get up, shuffle around a few steps, later in the day a few more. Three days later a transfer to the treatment ward, a room of her own. It had two beds, two dressers, but no room mate.

"My name's Sophie, I'll be your counselor." The voice belonged to a short, heavyset woman with much gray in her black hair, a wide Indian face.

"How long do I have to stay here?" Felice probed Sophie for some expression, some clue.

"Do you feel you can function? Out there? Right now?"

"I don't know."

"When you know we can talk about it."

"Am I under arrest?"

"No, this is a treatment facility. For alcoholism, drug addiction. You can walk out any time."

Felice thought that over. "I feel shaky."

Sophie nodded. "I know how it feels. I've been where you are."

Surprise. This nicely dressed, respectable, middle-aged woman? Who seemed so collected, so together? But she was stern, too.

"Come see me whenever you want, so long as I'm not with another patient. Your regular hour with me is at 10."

"Tomorrow?"

"And every other day."

"How long?"

"Until you are ready."

Two men playing a board game in the common room were in a heated argument. "The Middle East is more strategic than Africa, you should of . . . " Three women were huddled in intimate, whispered conversation in a corner. A few solitaries were sprinkled about. Every race, every age, in this microcosm of society. Felice felt alienated, alone, a random ion in a nuclear reactor.

A bell marked time for group. After lunch there would be individual counseling, then another group. Felice drifted along.

By the second week the fog began to lift. She knew where she was, had been told how she arrived. The several days in the detox ward were a blank.

"How come you don't say you're alcoholic? Or addict?" one of the men in group challenged. "You think you're better'n us?"

"No. So I've got a problem. So what. Doesn't mean I'm an alcoholic," Felice defended.

"Bullshit. They find you in a ditch. You're full of booze and drugs, and all you got is a problem. Well, welcome. We all here got the same problem. You're in denial."

She opened up more in individual counseling sessions. Sophie, motherly master of tough love, broke down the resistance.

"I worked the streets too." That seemed incongruous coming from this kind, middle-aged woman.

"I never . . . "

"Weren't you arrested? Twice?"

"Couldn't have been, I'd never . . ."

Sophie waved a copy of the arrest record. "That you?"

Felice stared at it. "Looks like me. Well, maybe . . . "

"Maybe?"

"Oh, all right, that's me. So it happened."

The third week in group she said, "My name's Felice and I'm an alcoholic." Shaking, weeping, and the others cheered and clustered around her, hugging her, laughing and crying.

"That's the beginning, that's the first step," the group leader said. "Now you can start to work."

She had to write her life story; then letters, letters, more letters: to her mother saying how she felt; to Landgraf, Rosalie, a teacher.

"Do I show them to you?" she said, clutching the sheaf of lined paper to her chest.

"Did you say what you felt? Sure? Get your feelings out on that paper?" Sophie's eyes, speaking love, gimlets boring in.

"Yeah. Sure. Mostly."

Sophie smiled. "OK. Burn them. Here. In this waste basket. That's putting the past behind you."

There was much paper. The smoke alarm blared claxon.

"Oh, shit," Sophie poured coffee on the blaze, slowing it down, and both laughed.

"Grab that pillow and put it on the floor. Now get down on your knees by it, fold your hands—no, don't lace fingers—and pretend that's somebody out of your past life towards whom you have anger. Pound on it. Scream, yell, cry. Go ahead."

Felice was self-conscious. It felt artificial, make-believe. The pillow was a shoe store clerk who had fondled her.

"Harder," Sophie rasped from the sidelines. "Put something into it. Pound it. Pound! That's better."

Through the metaphor of the pillow she vented anger that turned into rage that turned into screams and then wracking sobs, the life-long rage having stopped the pain.

Again and again. In the privacy of Sophie's soundproofed office. Memories came back, clear picture recall.

"Not my fault," Sophie said. "Say it. Louder. Like you believe it. Come on, I want to hear something I can believe. I was born a beautiful baby, say it. I was lovable. Not my fault my parents weren't there to love me. Good. Now pick up that blanket and roll it up. Sit in that rocking chair. Pretend that blanket is little Felice, the baby. Tell her. TELL HER! Tell her it wasn't her fault. Tell her you'll love and protect her. That's your little girl, that's your self locked inside of you. Only you can take care of her."

And Felice enfolded the blanket and crooned to it, reassured it, told it all she had never been told, and wept as she did until she was exhausted and no tears were left.

"Now you're working," Sophie said.

Bit by small bit, with backsliding at times, Felice grew stronger, clearer, her core integrating.

"No church? No religion?" Sophie asked, some time into the second month.

"I'm Indian," Felice looked sullen.

"Everybody needs some kind of spiritual connection," Sophie bored in. "Life on earth didn't start the day we were born. It won't end when we die. What does being Indian mean?"

"I dunno." A little girl voice.

"Want to find out?"

Felice nodded.

"Ever had teachings? Been in a sweat? A woman's full moon ceremony? No? Anybody ever tell you what it means to be a woman, what the monthly time is? The great gift, the power, given us? I'll help you learn."

When Felice enrolled at the State College on a tribal scholarship no one begrudged her. It was comparable to the all-expenses-paid relocation program of an earlier day when the BIA furnished travel money and housing to move Indians to the cities. Folks signed up for the free vacation, visited relatives, and came home when tired of the metropolitan noise, congestion, and prejudice. Another day, another program; now it was a college education. Same thing.

"Notice how they give out scholarships with tribal elections coming up," somebody said, a prosaic statement not a question.

"Wasting it on her, she been gone years too."

"They say she's smart, been through treatment. Don't drink no more."

The hard core was unspoken. There had been rumors of drug dealing, being a mule for Mexican shippers, of prostitution. Then stories about her crashing from drug use, alcohol, being hauled out of the gutter into detox and treatment. From treatment to traditional ways, the sweat lodge, then ever deeper into . . . into . . . that's when even the rumors stopped. Christians were silent; for generations they'd been told the old ways were tools of the devil, evil and anti-Christ. Traditionalists kept quiet; it was improper to talk about these things. The net result was silence. Everyone knew, no one talked. Felice was becoming a spiritual woman, a leader. People were watching.

Then they talked about other things, Felice's sobriety and going to college were not all that important, and neither were the elections. All that tribal council business was just a sham, the real decision makers were never out front but those quiet, hidden polarizations revolving around men and women whose views and judgments accumulated respect.

Felice seemed quieter, more centered. She rented a new, small reservation house in a clump of replanted pine, was ready when the share-the-ride car came for her for the 35-mile ride, and she lived alone. She looked the same but there was something about her bearing that when she walked to the store no cars made bootlegger turns to pick her up.

"Boozhoo." David looked up from his desk. "How's the school girl?"

"Fine. How's the tribal lawyer?"

"Fine too. You want to sue somebody? Have a legal problem?"

Head and shoulders said no. "That coffee fresh or from yesterday?"

"I hear you made the Dean's List again." David's feet were on his desk and he handed the brimful cup as though it contained radioactive isotopes. "Next thing I know you'll be in law school and ready to go into partnership."

"Maybe teach. Don't know yet. I like kids." Her face lit in a half-smile. "I didn't have much mothering when I was little. Maybe I want to feed the little child inside me, the one had such a hard time growing up."

David waited. He knew she would get around to it sooner or later.

"Whatever happened to that Ruth?" she asked.

"Same as your social worker. We split. She's doing corporation law with her daddy's firm. Ever hear from him?"

Her eyes said no. "I thought about it. Trying to find him. Nobody knows where he is and I can't relive my past, don't want to."

David thought about it a while. "It was different for me," he finally said. "I was dumped too, but it was Dad being drunk and Mom killed in the accident when he was driving, and then he just went to the Cities and never came back, until he got shot and laid on a railroad track."

"I know." She sat in silence. "So you stayed away from the booze by and large."

"Most of the time," he laughed. "What really happened to you, you're so changed? It wasn't all the treatment, was it?"

"That started it, at the rehab. That was tough at first. You know, I hit bottom pretty hard, took me two months to get through rehab; most people make it in four weeks. This older woman who ran the program, we became friends. She took me into sweats, into women's pipe group, ceremonies, things like that. After a while memories came back. That was hard, didn't want to believe it. But she helped me work through."

David shook his head in commiseration.

"Takes a long time," Felice said. "Still working on it. You don't shake all those years of being one personality to being another overnight. The sweats, the traditional ways, that helps."

"Didn't know there was much of the old traditional stuff around any more," David remarked. "Thought it ended with my grandpa and others his age."

"It's still going, maybe coming back some." She hesitated, shifted gears. "There any law says things taken from Indians have to be returned? Religious items, like that, in museums?" Felice asked.

"I think so, never had to deal with it so I'm not up on the law. Why do you want to know?"

Felice's eyes flicked away, then back to David. "I was browsing in one of those old Smithsonian Annual Reports in the library the other day, the Ethnology Reports . . . "

"Those big olive ones?"

She nodded. "There was a footnote, I don't even know why I looked at that, said somebody was sent here in the 1880s and took back a bunch of stuff."

"Nothing new about that," David frowned, "they hauled away everything they could including the bones." Felice could be exasperating at times; David was sure she had something specific in mind but was taking her time coming around to it.

"Next time you're in Washington," she pursued, "could you take time and check it out?"

"I could try. What is it we're looking for? There are bound to be boxes and boxes. I don't even know if they will let me look at the stuff. Pipes? Drums? Beadwork? What?"

Felice fidgeted. "I'll try to find out. When's your next trip?"

She knew, he was sure she knew, but she wasn't saying. "Week after next," he said. "Call or stop in before, or it'd be a waste of time."

She called and he came to her house, surprised by the neatness of it, taken aback by the decor. They sat on floor cushions because there was little furniture. Floral pattern beadwork hung on the walls—bandoleers, sashes, aprons. From one kitchen wall hung drying bundles of sage, twists of sweetgrass, and lining the back of one kitchen counter were jars with porcupine quills, Indian tea, and herbs.

"Your beading?" he asked.

She nodded. "Therapy." They drank tea.

She extended a package of tobacco but held onto it. "I'd like to ask you to do something special. Two things really. Back around 1910 Frances Densmore came through here and recorded some of the old people singing. Many midewin songs . . . "

"The old religious society?"

"That's right."

"I'd like you to go to the Library of Congress and get a copy of those recordings and bring it back. You know, a record or a tape."   Felice, centered, was following the beat of an inner drum. "The second request is that you go to the Smithsonian and find out about the things this Hoffman took away from here, if they still have them, and what they are. They belong here. They're sacred."

David stared at his cousin. "You'd better tell me more about all this."

It was some time in the telling, the results of her piecing together bits of information from the college library with the fragments of remembered stories and anecdotes from Rosalie, Great Uncle Peter, and others.

"The songs, that's simple," she said. "The college music department has a phonograph record from the Library of Congress. On the jacket there's a description of Densmore making the rounds of the reservations when wax cylinder recording first came out in the early 1900s. She made it a point to record the old people's singing. One of the places she came was here. Around 1911 I think."

"Simple enough," David said. "Now who and what is Hoffman?"

"All I know is from a part of a paragraph in the Annual Report from, let's see, 1885. I copied it out for you. It says he was sent out here to investigate something from Henry Schoolcraft's journals that said we had picture writing that was more developed than the Egyptian hieroglyphics. And he came out here and brought back samples and other objects, a big collection taken from the old people here. He was going to write a big report on it, but our library here doesn't have it."

David mulled that. "Doesn't make much sense. Schoolcraft was at Mackinack in the 1840s and took one trip through here to the source of the Mississippi. We had to show him where it was."

"He was also married to the granddaughter of Waubojeeg, and his mother-in-law told him a lot," Felice pointed out.

"Yeah, yeah, and Longfellow got his Indian legends and the basis of the Hiawatha story from Schoolcraft, what else is new?"

"OK, so it took the Smithsonian 40 years to follow up on it, but it says this Hoffman brought the stuff back and I want you to find out if he did, and where it is, and what it is," she pouted.

David stood. "Cut the bullshit, Felice. What's it all about? Really?"

"Oh, sit down. You're acting like a lawyer."

"Well, I am a lawyer and you're asking me to do something, so lay it all out." David paced up and down.

"All right already. Sit down, will you, you make me nervous hovering over me like that. OK. There used to be birchbark scrolls with picture writing on them . . . "

"We never had a written language," David snapped. "All the books tell you that."

"We did. It was picture writing. Pictographs. More. Each picture, or drawing, stood for a whole idea, a teaching. It was ideographs, not just pictographs."

"A little ochre drawing on a rock somewhere."

"No," Felice insisted. "There's more to it than that. Now listen. Panels of birchbark were sewn together into a long strip and covered with hundreds of tiny ideographs. Some scrolls told the legends of our migration from the east coast to Minnesota. Others were . . . "

"Well?"

"Instructions. Details on the teachings and initiations into each of the four levels of midewin. And there were smaller ones too, that told specific events, or the words for songs."

"How do you know all that?" David pointed a finger at her in unconscious courtroom manner.

"Don't point! That's rude! I found some stuff at the library and zeroxed it for you, and there's one book by some Canadian who mentions Hoffman. I checked that out for you to take along, but bring it back or it's my neck at school. And I've been at some teachings where they've drawn ideographs on sand, and the teacher uses those as memory devices for the oral tradition, both for the teacher and those of us who're learning."

"Are you into this midewin?" David was incredulous.

Felice hesitatingly said, "Yes."

"I'll do it." David took the tobacco.

Two weeks later he went to the Library of Congress, expecting little, but was welcomed warmly and shown to the Folklore Section.

"Oh, we don't sell those records any more," a staffer told him. "Haven't for years. They only contained a small part of the wax cylinder recordings anyhow."

A dead end, as David expected.

"Is there any way of listening to the cylinders, or taping them?" He was making conversation.

"That's not possible," he was told. "They're too fragile. We gathered them here for safe storage. Some were at Archives, some at the Smithsonian, some here. It took us months to record them on tape."

"You mean, you have them on tape?" Bingo!

"It's a set of 18 tapes, about 15 hours of Ojibwe music. We can copy a set for you in our sound studio. The cost is, let's see, a little over $800."

Shot down again.

"We did make a complete set for each reservation two years ago, at the completion of the preservation project. You're from Mahng Lake you say, well, they should have one. That's one of the places where Densmore recorded. I'm sure they received one."

He called Felice that evening.

"That tribal council is such a mess they couldn't find their own bellybuttons," she said.

"Well, go over and ask. Look. Besides, my office isn't all that bad."

"Almost, and it isn't there or you'd have known," she replied. "You look for them when you get back. You know your way around that place. Probably came and somebody put it on a shelf or in a file. What about the Hoffman stuff?"

"Tomorrow. I'll be going to the Smithsonian tomorrow."

A security guard ushered David from the information booth to the cluttered maze of the Anthropology and Archeology Department, where he was quizzed about what he wanted to see, and why. He gave a lame explanation which was greeted with silence and raised eyebrows. Several of the staff were Indian, including the head of the department, who was a stocky young Dakota woman with a doctorate and (he later found out) a national reputation.

"It's in the attic," she finally said. "Asbestos country. Most of our material is stored, we don't have staff or space. You'll have to wear protective clothing and we'll send somebody with you."

"I'm sure I can manage." David did not want to be monitored.

"It's locked area," she said firmly, and a husky young man interning at the museum accompanied him.

Up several flights, through locked doors, farther and farther away from the public displays. At the last doorway David had to slip on disposable booties and cotton gloves. He raised his eyebrows at the gloves, and his companion explained, "Oil and sweat on your hands could get on the items."

The door opened into a room filled with wooden cupboards, each containing wide drawers.

"Shakers in the top three drawers, then going down are hand drums, sashes, and so on." The intern glanced at an inventory sheet and back at the numbered drawers, "From then on it's birchbark scrolls."

"Scrolls," David said.

There were three drawers full. Hoffman must have been persuasive to have obtained so many.

Small strips of bark, about three inches wide by ten to twelve inches long, contained what looked like dancing stick figures, seven or eight to a strip.

"Song scrolls," the guide said. "Tell the word content of a song. Maybe indicate the tune judging from the up and down position of the figures. I don't know much about them. Nobody's been into these for ages."

Layers of dust coated the bark strips. He learned later that they were called Song Boards and had been used by mide teachers, instructing initiates to take them home and learn the songs they had to know by the time of the next ceremonies.

"This one's different." David picked it up gingerly. It was tinted red as though a child had crayoned over the scribed contents.

"What's the number? On the back." The guide checked his sheet. "Shows a battle between Sioux and Ojibwe on the ice at Red Lake. Red coloring indicates importance of the scroll, it says here."

David replaced it. "Look at that, here are some in tatters, crumbling. One has disintegrated completely!"

"No money, no restorers. It's too bad, but we have many compartments like this one." The guide closed the drawer, pulled out another completely and put it on the work table in the center of the room.

Here they were. Almost two feet wide and up to six feet long. David gasped as he and the guide carefully unfurled the first. It was covered with hundreds of precise, artful drawings scribed into the brownish back of the birchbark. The top and bottom of the scroll were fastened to basswood strips, and the four individual panels making up the scroll had been fastidiously stitched, probably with basswood fiber.

A migration scroll recorded the major events and legends of centuries of the Ojibwe migration from east coast to central Minnesota. David recognized Otter Woman, the Great Medicine Bear, and other events from his cramming the night before in his hotel room.

"It ends at Bear Island on Leech Lake," he murmured to himself.

"They all do," the guide said. "All the migration scrolls. Even those they found in Canada. They all end at Bear Island. Don't know why."

Some of the ideographs were crosshatched, others in outline.

David wished he knew more, knew the significance of the difference and the meanings.

"If a panel wore out, it would be copied and sewn into the scroll as a replacement," Felice had said. All of the panels on this scroll looked to be the same age, as did the stitching.

"My God, this is a whole new art form," David exclaimed as they unrolled the next scroll and he faced its entirety of hundreds of crosshatched figures, rectangular patterns, and curving lines. "Not new at all," he corrected himself. "Just unknown. Maybe it was supposed to be unknown, except to the mide priests."

They weighted down the long scroll at each end to keep it from curling on itself. The largest elements were four rectangles indicating the initiation lodges for the four progressive degrees of the midewin. Tiny figures indicated where the teachers sat, and where the initiates. Small footsteps showed the paths to be followed by the initiates in walking through the obstacles and pitfalls of life to a better way of living. Other figures indicated the spirit helpers, some in the form of animals. The complexity was bewildering.

One large scroll was so hard and brittle they did not dare unroll it. "We'd have to humidify it to soften it," the guide remarked. "Don't have the time or equipment. By rights they should be stored flat, not rolled up, between two sheets of glass or something. Don't have space either."

"How? How did this man get these things?" David asked, awed by what he was seeing.

"It's explained in his article in the Report."

"We don't have that at home."

They went to the Anthropology Library where a cheerful little grayhaired woman found it. "Volume 7. 1885-6. Actually published in 1891. An anomaly, they probably missed putting out an annual report some years. I gather that Hoffman did his field work at your reservation around 1885. Here is what you are looking for." She handed him the volume, saying, "We have a copying machine you can use."

"But . . . this is over 150 pages. And I might damage the book!"

"You're right. Well, you can use space here and read, make notes, whatever." At the end of the extensive, illustrated report Hoffman explained that the older Indians, fearing the complete destruction of the Indian ways and midewin in particular had given him the information and the objects so as to preserve them.

David left the Smithsonian and sat on a Mall park bench in a daze. All assumptions about his heritage, his forebears, his culture had had a violent, cataclysmic jolt. I am not who I thought I was, I come from a people more sophisticated, more complex than I was ever told. Or had I been? Had it been hinted, suggested, shown by examples to which I'd been blinded by school, church, society? Did Felice know when she asked me to search?

On the stopover in Minneapolis he taxied to Lien's rare book store downtown. He scrutinized the high shelf of oversized volumes and found several of the olive Annual Reports, but none with the magic Vol. 7 on the spine. Too much to hope for.

"Some don't have the volume number embossed on the spine," Mr. Lien said. "Let's look again. Ah, here is one. A little damaged, we'll take that into account pricing it."

Felice listened without interrupting, the still-wrapped book between them on the floor.

"I have an idea how Hoffman got the scrolls," David concluded. "When he arrived here the word was out the rez would be allotted, everybody expected it. That's what was happening everywhere. And here were the old timers caught in a vise. On one side the BIA was punishing them for practicing the old religion—you know about the rulebook for the agents telling them to withold 30 days' rations from religious practitioners and their families, and for the second offense to withold food 30 days plus 30 days in jail—and on the other side the missionaries threatened eternal hellfire and damnation. Now with allotment coming the end was in sight. So they gave up the sacred scrolls and some of the information. Except in 1889 allotment was voted down here, the only place it was defeated."

"Maydway," Felice said.

"What?"

"The old chief who rallied opposition to allotment. He was in his 80s then. Maydwaygwanoning. He Who Is Spoken To. Your great-great-granduncle. Mine too. They had seven treaty sessions and each time he rallied the people to vote it down. That's why our reservation is intact, and all the others were allotted and most of the land lost. Maydway . . . "

Who would have guessed one old man had so much tenacity in him? Who would have guessed the young woman had inherited this trait? And she had been quiet about it, so very quiet, a motionless hunter waiting hours for the sure shot.

"I did find the tapes," he said almost incidentally. "They were in a beautiful leather case in a corner of the chairman's office. He didn't know what they were. What'll we do with them?"

"There's a lady at the college communications center will dub copies if we provide clean tapes," Felice said. "Let's see, eighteen tapes to a set, eleven sets, makes 198 cassettes, that's about $400 at discount. How you fixed for money?"

David shrugged. "Why eleven sets?"

"Why not?" She didn't feel like saying four directions and seven grandfathers makes eleven. "It's a good number is all. Eleven. I'll go halves with you."

"Okay. Who gets them?"

"I don't know. Those who should." Drumcarriers. Mide who carried the Little Boy Water Drums and would respect the gift.

David guessed she had recipients in mind and might, or might not, talk about it some other time. He pointed at the book on the floor between them.

She fetched a large abalone shell and other items, then sat on the floor again. She spread a red cloth and placed the still-wrapped book on it, then shredded dried sage leaves into the shell, the megis. She lit the sage and wafted the incense over David and over herself with an eagle feather. From a small leather pouch she extracted the separately-wrapped pipestem and bowl, passed them over the curling smoke. She filled the bowl with semas and did the filling of the bowl carefully, painstakingly, a tiny pinch at a time, each pinch offered in the right way. She lit the pipe, blowing the smoke in the four directions, and handed the pipe to David, who inhaled once and returned it to her for completion.

When she was done with her prayers Felice picked up the package. "What is in here was given away in good faith for safekeeping. It is now coming back home. What is still away that should not be, we will do our best to bring back home."

They sat quietly. The smoldering sage collapsed into ash but the solacing scent was still about.

So that stalwart old man Maydwaygwanoning was the pivot, the fulcrum on whom events turned, David thought. He thwarted the theft of the land, the latrociny of the old ways, which no one could have predicted. Had the scrolls and the songboards been surrendered prematurely? The point was moot; what counted was that they still existed and that somehow, sometime they would be coming home, home at last.

He knew also there would be a public role for him to play in the bureaucratic games that would ensue, the political and the legal gymnastics, and that he would do it, but that the real decision making, the real leadership would come from the shadow cabinet of opinion-molders, the jessakid seers into things like Felice.

"Migwetch," Felice said as she picked up the book and held it aloft in her nearest-the-heart left hand, and then slowly and with great care unwrapped it. The book fell open to a full-page detailed drawing of one of the great scrolls, and she let the book lie on the floor like that, open, like a mide teacher's sand drawing for initiates, and said once more, "Migwetch, Maydway."

Migwetch, Felice, David thought, marveling at the healing and growing in his cousin. Then he said it aloud and she smiled. They both smiled. And it was good.

She said it in Indian, and then in English, "All my family."

Felice had come home.

RITES

C arl Bartoldy was a white man without a tribe who found a home for his soul in the Indian world of the Upper Midwest. Brought up in a city family of agnostics with no ethnic focus, he had lost what few bearings he had as an eighteen-year-old in Viet Nam. He was not of an analytical bent and could not have explained why his estilled spiritual gyroscope resumed humming among the traditional hospitality, open generosity, and holistic lifeview of the Indians. He was not the first white whose inner life rebounded under such tutelage. Over the centuries there had been captives, traders, trappers, voyageurs and others who refused return, preferring to stay in the orbit of Indian civilization. They found a spiritual base here that had eluded them in that other world or had been destroyed there. The hill people of the Golden Triangle had saved Carl's life and sown the seed.

He had moments of semiconsciousness, not even aware of being in a Hmong hut on a dirt floor pallet in the hill country succored by the Montagnards.

"I killed the boy!" he screamed, convulsed in spasms when he wrapped his arms tightly about his chest, his body jerking on the floor before relapsing into coma in what looked like a grand mal seizure. At the end he collapsed into a fetal clump. He was a boy himself who shaved only occasionally. "The boy, the child, I shot him! I killed a child!"

They did not understand English. It was early in the war before the Hmong had been co-opted and armed by the American CIA as they had been once before, on a smaller scale, by the French. A small group of men hunting monkeys with crossbows had found him unconscious in the jungle with blood loss from a nasty wound in the right thigh and carried him to their village on an improvised litter. They had not seen anyone else around. A bloody trail and broken branches on the jungle floor showed he had crawled there from somewhere and collapsed.

In later years he had memory glimpses of that time: an elderly shaman praying, singing over him, treating the wound gently with an herbal poultice, other men and women in the background; strange, loud music, gongs and tinkling little cymbals or bells; people having a feast outside the hut and bringing him stew-like meat; being tied to a litter and carried uphill to another village. Each time he woke he would yell about the boy he had shot, and then convulse. His caretakers would hug, stroke, and comfort him, speaking gently, and again there was chanting and music until he passed out again.

The elders had talked about the situation and decided to move him to the more remote village higher up. The war was moving closer, why ask for trouble should they be found caring for a combatant. They had fought Chinese, Laotians, Vietnamese for centuries and maintained their independence in the mountains by dint of a warrior ethos, but one thing learned from generations of war was picking and choosing a battleground, and the little agricultural village in the low hill country was not such a place.

The times of consciousness became longer and he was brought outside the new hut to sit in the sun and watch the children play. He marvelled at the endless patience and affection shown the youngsters. Every adult seemed uncle or aunt to each child, encouraging, praising, correcting, stroking, petting, and holding, until Carl could not tell who was the parent and who was not. There were frequent feasts amid gongs, bells, loud shouts and chants and strange music. Carl thought they were parties, social events drawing most clan members in the area. In fact some were celebrations for the naming of a newborn, and others were animal sacrifices, part of healing rituals. One such was to bring healing to Carl, but he could not understand what was being said to him or know that the food served him came from animals sacrificed that he might heal.

Communication was by motions, pointing, signs, each speaking his own language which the other could not understand. Carl still had episodes when the killing memory overcame him and he convulsed into a rigid fetus, unable to cope with the horror and his remorse.

"He poked out of the brush as we came by, my partner and I, on a long range reconnaissance," Carl said. "His first shot killed my partner, then he and I shot at the same time and he got me in the leg. I got him in the chest. A child. Just a child." He had never killed before and would never do so again; it was too much like killing himself, an emotionally abandoned child miscast as a soldier/killer. There was a buried memory which never emerged into Carl's consciousness and therefore he could not understand his driven, irresistible frenzy. As a young child he had overheard his mother telling someone about having had an abortion and had drawn the mistaken conclusion that he was supposed to have died, was not worth birthing, but had somehow emerged into life through an incomprehensible error. Killing the Viet Cong boy linked with this unrecognized, subconscious cancer. He wept, not understanding it at all, and the shaman comforted him striving for return of Carl's soul to his seemingly epileptic body from the spirit world whence it had been transported. What western civilization considered unscientific superstition was not off the mark at all.

When the crying stopped the shaman pointed at the sky, circling his hand and arm and bringing it down to circle and envelop Carl, then laying the flat palm on the ground and holding it there before shaking Carl's hand. He did this whenever Carl had such spells, and gradually Carl took it to mean that when he rolled on the earth grasping himself in the agony of his remorse a spirit would come and help him recover. Carl thought this was a good, a lovely thing. But it was a misunderstanding. The Hmong shaman thought that Carl had epilepsy, a sacred affliction. He was saying that when the spirit catches you, you fall down. At those times the soul leaves the body to commune with the spirits, returning enriched and perhaps gifted to become a shaman and able to help those who were ill or suffering or needed intercession with the spirit world, having himself been there.

In time Carl healed and learned a few words of the difficult Hmong language and some of the customs of his hosts. He felt liked, a participant in feasts and ceremonies although he understood little of what was being said or done, puzzled that he was invited and propelled to the forefront at such times and to visit the sick, though he did not fathom what was expected of him and all he could do was to say a few words in English and to hug and stroke the afflicted as he had seen done with others and as had been done to him, which seemed to gratify his hosts. Eventually an American patrol came to the village and took him back, to a hospital, to the States and civilian life, and he thought of his time with the short and stocky dark-skinned tribesmen and their strange ways with gratitude and fondness. Beyond saving his life they had somehow stimulated a spiritual antenna that would eventually enhance and enrich it. However the first several civilian years, some spent in haphazard pursuit of education, were a time of drug use, alcoholism, and madness from which he emerged painfully and slowly, spending several months in a VA hospital and then in a halfway house.

He worked, in that other world, at a job in town he liked well enough, teaching design and drafting at the technical college; summers he supervised tribal housing construction and taught building skills to previously unemployed tribal members; but the inner life that is the wellspring of it all, that secret garden, that hidden valley, that Shangri La which is at the core had come to identify itself as Indian over the years. Outwardly there was aesthetic pleasure as well; he found dark-skinned, dark-haired people attractive, an echo perhaps of a childhood aunt with black hair and dark skin whose love and gentle acceptance of him was a ray of sunshine in his youth.

At home with his Native American wife they opened the door to their children, hoping they would take to the spiritual path of the Red Road but never forcing or pushing. Carl had been embraced, taken in especially by the older Indian people, taught to put down his tobacco offering and pray daily, a token to, an acknowledgment of the great mystery, showing how Real People give themselves to living as part of the whole of creation wherein everything had a role, a function, a spiritual essence: trees, rocks, earth, any and all living creatures, every breath of breeze, each drop of rain or flake of snow.

And so it happened that his daughter learned about the yearlong berry fast upon coming into her first time, that the sons learned about the feast for the first-killed deer and giving away all the meat to the elderly and the poor, about fasting for the life vision; that they entered the sweat lodge standing a little ways from the house; that Carl gave away more than he took; that his heart cheered and he put down tobacco thanks when the eagle, Migizi, circled overhead as a sign that he walked in beauty and lived in harmony.

When Carl brought in the last bag of weekly groceries, he had a bouquet of flowers, their bright colors the pied hope of better times in what had been dreary weeks. He had at least remembered the flowers, but there was something else he was supposed to have gotten that still eluded him.

"Oh, nice," Melissa said. "For Mom. What's the occasion?"

"For you." He spoke quietly, having come to the speechways of the people, a way relying on understatement and assumed understandings. Woodland Ojibwe language was soft and flowing while the Dakota prairie language was sharper, staccato in comparison; in the forests quiet was essential while in the plains distances, being heard was more important. Not many people still spoke it and Carl had difficulty learning it. A construction accident long ago had diminished his hearing and he was unable to distinguish verbal nuances. He had a few words and phrases, and understood more than he spoke, but it was a limited command of a beautiful and complex language which had its own unique ways of expressing thought, a differently constructed logic from the European. In the 18th century it was considered the American equivalent of diplomatic French, a continental *lingua franca*.

The girl gazed at the flowers in wonder.

"Me? How come?" She had never been given flowers by anyone in all her fourteen years.

"Celebrate."

"Celebrate what?"

"Womanhood. Mum says you've come on your first time. Says she got you started on berry fast. Wanted you to know I'm happy for you coming into woman power. Beautiful. So're you. Beautiful." He turned abruptly and left to do chores, feeling awkward, unsure how much to say; this was the stuff of woman talk. He did not want to embarrass the girl, but he did want her to know his feelings. He went outside looking for Joel to help the boy with his last minute preparations, but the truck was gone, so Joel had gone ahead without him. All right, it was the boy's responsibility to get everything ready, but Carl could not help feeling left out, as he had been all along through the prolonged, intimate teachings and preparations between Uncle Viborg and Joel. In his childhood days he had heard women talking about their monthly periods as "the curse". He preferred the Indian teaching that it was not only a regular sloughing of tissue and ova no longer viable, but the creator's proof of the gift to women to bear new life. The monthly time made the woman, already powerful, even more so. That is why she stayed by herself, did not cook or do dishes for others, why the men's pipes were kept wrapped when she was around, lest she unwittingly weaken the men. A powerful teaching.

Before feeding and watering the horses he stood at the glacially-rilled boulder where he prayed daily and put down his tobacco. "Thank you for the beautiful daughter you have given us," he said at the end of his regular prayer. "Help her cherish her womanhood and respect it. Help her value the gift and the power you have given her."

Melissa stood in the middle of the kitchen clasping the flowers. She feasted on the colors and inhaled the delicate smells, put them in a quart jar on the kitchen table. She hoped they would last long. In her imagination she saw a butterfly circling the bouquet and coming to rest on a yellow flower, opening and closing its lovely orange and black wings. The butterfly rose, circled the flowers, and flew away as childhood was leaving her. Mixed feelings of sadness, pride and anticipation filled her, knowledge of new responsibilities coming her way.

The pickup truck skidded into the yard. Carl shook his head; Joel had a heavy foot on the gas. Funny. Joel was the careful, responsible one about schoolwork, keeping appointments, structuring and organizing his life. Behind the wheel of a vehicle his only speed was fast. Younger Kit was harum scarum, sloppy, and disorganized, but a sensible driver. Now where was the logic, the consistency, in that? But then, where did it say life had to be logical? There was no procedure manual directing how life was to be.

"Where are you going with that sheet of plywood? he called to Joel's back as the boy loaded it.

"Uncle Viborg says I have to build a scaffold. I'll bring it back after." Carl wondered if he would ever see it again.

"D'you bring the rope?" Joel asked, his arms now loaded with hammer, nails, and tools from the workshop.

That's what he had forgotten! "Never mind," Joel said. "I'll borrow the clothesline."

That's old rope, Carl wanted to say. It's broken several times and I've had to reknot it. But Joel was hurried, frantically getting ready what he had deferred to the last minute and Carl kept quiet.

"Guess that's all," Joel said. "Everything else is over there. You coming for the truck later on this evening? Uncle said no one's to come out to where I'll be once I . . . "

Carl knew that, knew that in putting the boy out to fast Uncle Viborg would check on him, that no one else could intrude or disturb someone on the spiritual pilgrimage, that dual sojourn within oneself and out into the mystery of life. He knew the boy would be somewhere back in the woods, at least a half mile or more from the river landing where the truck would be.

"I'll be getting it," Carl said. He wanted to say much more. I love you. I hope you find what you are searching for. I hope you'll be safe, that going without food and water won't be too hard on you. I know you undertake the hardships and suffering in pursuing your spiritual quest and also in behalf of all the people. I wish I could be with you, could have put you out though I know that has to be done by an uncle or other elderly teacher. I wish I could still call you by your baby name, but now you're taller and stronger than I am and going off on your great journey. He turned away as the boy leaped into the cab and roared off. From the kitchen window Melissa watched, not so wrapped in her own mystery that she was not aware that her brother was engaging in his own.

Later Carl walked to the river landing before dusk. The pines were candling, new growth reaching upward, and the swamp dogwood that people called red willow sparkled redder bark than it had in winter. There were fresh imprints of deer hooves in the grass and Carl looked for tiny fawn signs; the newborns would be barely a month old, but beginning to venture out. He did not see any.

At the river the empty truck was waiting. The boy had evidently put it in four-wheel drive and taken it across the meadow and up the hills toward the tall pine grove, about where Carl thought he would go. He saw Joel and Uncle Viborg in conversation a little ways off, near the cottage which Joel had claimed for his own, an uninsulated shell adequate enough in temperate weather but impossible after the first frost. Joel, between childhood and adult independence, still came home for most meals even while "living alone." Carl`s impulse was to join the boy and the uncle, but he knew they needed privacy to go over the last of the instructions, putting the eagle feather up on the cabin roof, the last food and drink and prayers. Before daybreak Joel would walk from his cabin to the scaffold in the woods alone, climb up and begin his fast with the rising of the sun, beginning the inward journey, occasionally using his hand drum to accompany the ancient chants and songs and the prayers Uncle Viborg had been teaching him. The boy had been hopelessly unmusical in school but had a clear, strong voice singing the difficult Ojibwe music that ranged from very high notes to low bass, a true sense of the musicality and a photographic memory for the language. "That's because he has something special to say, to offer," Uncle Viborg commented once, "he's been given a special gift."

Now the boy seemed to be listening intently as Uncle Viborg spoke earnestly, gesticulating. They paid no attention to Carl, who climbed into the truck and drove home.

He woke with a startled reflex before daylight. There was only a hint of graying and Carl was wide awake, long before the alarm clock would have roused him. His first thought was of the boy trudging through the wet morning grass on his sojourning quest, anticipating the dawn. He would be up on his scaffold before daylight. Carl tried to go back to sleep but it evaded him. He rose, debated going to the landing, but worried about intruding, decided not to. He smudged himself with sage smoke and offered his tobacco. Once at a powwow he heard tourists say "that smells like pot" as a dancer was smudging himself before entering the ring. Carl wanted to say to them, "That's not pot. That's sage, a sacred medicine used to purify oneself." But by then he had become sufficiently acculturated that directly contradicting someone was taboo.

"Don't worry so about the boy," Thelberta said after dinner. "The spirits'll watch over him. He'll be all right."

That night he was restless. Unable to sleep, he got up again and went outside in his pajamas, checking the weather. A gusty breeze had come up, harbinger of storm. The daytime winds usually quieted at night; this one could mean harsh weather.

I shouldn't worry so, Carl chided himself. Joel had camped out in below-zero weather, at first to see if he could do it, then for the joy of it. He was tough and strong. He could handle himself. He had hunted, run a trap line, canoed north of the Arctic Circle. Carl told himself all this repeatedly and finally lapsed into restless half-sleep.

His first waking thought was that Joel would now be thirsty, feeling the first hunger spasms. Perhaps he would feel morning chills in the damp air before the dew burned off. It was still gusting but the sky was clear. Odd weather. The boy had been so intent on obtaining a vision, a clear signal of what his life course should be. Would a bear appear at the fasting place, as it had for a family friend one year? Would a timber wolf show itself, as it had for Carl once, or a goshawk another time, or eagles as they had several times? What would it mean if one did? The context as much as the behavior would enable Uncle Viborg to interpret the significance.

Carl took the woods trail to the landing. He would not approach closely or disturb the fast, but he wanted a sense of approximately where the boy was, some reassuring sign he was all right.

"Uncle'll be watching out for him," his wife had said to the retreating back. "It's for him to do. Don't be coming near!"

He knew all that and waved acknowledgment as he went out. Thelberta had been put out to fast several times, once in broiling sun, making it for several days in the little ground shelter she had had to construct of bent poles covered with a tarpaulin that was just large enough to provide cover when she slept or sat up. Other women were fasting nearby and the elderly aunt had checked on each of them daily, starting the second day at noon. Finding the women together on one of her checks, the aunt sternly sent them back to their own shelters. It was supposed to be a time for meditation and prayer.

Carl's own fasts had been solitary occasions and he had gone out by himself, no one to put him out or check on him; being adopted

Indian by birth or blood made Carl reluctant to ask or make demands even by implication. That made no sense, Thelberta had said, but it was a boundary he had set for himself in the ambiguous territory between the Indian and non-Indian worlds, and he did not want to risk rejection. He went out like that at least once a year, sometimes more often, leaving the house long before daybreak and climbing a tree to watch the sunrise. He would return late at night. These one-day fasts were not so much vision quests as a time dedicated to inner search and outer connection to creation. He became aware of all the animals, the earth and the sky, sun and stars, and his place within creation as the earth's spin on its axis created the illusion that it was the sun that was rising and setting when in fact it was the whirling of the globe in the universe with Carl on it that made it all happen.

At the landing Carl pulled one of the small wooden benches close to the crescent-moon-shaped altar within whose arms he had built many fires for sweats. The bare framework of the sweat lodge stood about twenty feet west of the altar. They had taken down the tarps to dry and store to prevent mildew and would place them over the domed poles before the next sweat. Being caretaker of the place and the lodge was a responsibility given to Carl years before by elders who had come to instruct him and Thelberta how to build it. There had been clear distinctions made what tasks fell to men, what to women. Men cut and erected the poles, women built the altar. Men made fires, heated the rocks and handed them in; women were responsible for the water. The newly built sweat lodge had to be blessed, dedicated by the elders who had instructed them in the building of it.

"You will be ashkabewis of this lodge," they had told him, "the caretaker. You will rebuild it in the spring every year, maybe move it a little ways when the ground has been used too much." Then they had called him to stand between the two points of the crescent and given him a name, his second one. The first had come at the time of adoption long ago.

"I dreamed this name for you last night," the name-giver had said. Carl had known the significance of the name instantly. The new name meant Beautiful Day and it had sprung from his joy of life, of the day, of the building of the sweat lodge and the hard work of the lengthy preparations. His eyes moistened from gratitude for the recognition, and because there had been so many years long ago when life had not been beautiful for him. It was reaffirmation that he belonged. The name was both recognition and a challenge, the setting of a value to live up to during hard times.

Carl saw no sign of Joel; he knew Uncle Viborg wasn't around because the uncle's pristine compact wasn't parked in the open spot away from the popple grove where most others would put theirs helter skelter. Uncle did not want sap dripping on the nice wax job, or birds to grace hood and roof with white splotches.

Carl was sure that Joel had found a spot downriver, probably near the hilltop where the river made a sharp turn, because the truck's tire tracks two days before had headed that way. There was a deep current at the bend; above and below the river was wider and could be waded. Just below the bend there was a small island where does retreated in spring to birthe fawns and hide them until they were grown enough to cross. By then they would also be able to scamper to safety from predators.

The longer Carl sat the clearer the sound of the water over the upstream rapids became. He heard and sometimes saw ducks in their restless feeding. Heard the Canada geese apparently nesting nearby. Saw the osprey patrolling for fish. Carl kept glancing downstream hoping in time to observe some sign of the boy's whereabouts. He noticed something white fluttering near the top of a large red pine on the downstream hilltop but could not make out what it was. A piece of windblown plastic? Carl knew the spot, crowned by hundred-year-old pines, a great stand of old trees 60 or 70 feet high. A puzzle, that white flag in a field of green.

Mallard drakes were having a splashing duel almost at Carl's feet, a common sport during this mating season, and the man smiled as he watched the hen watching the ritual maneuver. Then it suddenly came to him what he had seen downstream and his heart pounded. The fluttering white high in the tree was from a blanket or a cloth. The boy had built his scaffold thirty feet or more off the ground and . . . and . . . that meant cross braces ten, twelve feet apart. Maybe more, because there was at least that much distance between trees. What had he used for the braces on which to build the platform? Saplings? The purloined plywood sheet for the platform itself? The rope? That rotting old clothesline to tie the braces to the red pines? And who ever heard of a fasting scaffold that high?

"I'm going to keep fire for him," he told Thelberta at home, packing a blanket, tarp, coffee thermos, and a jacket.

She made to speak, reconsidered, thinking it would not be the first time someone had sought to give support and strengthening prayers to a person on fast by keeping a parallel vigil some distance away, offering tobacco, cedar, other medicines, and above all, prayers.

Carl built a fire inside the arms of the altar, as he would have had there been a sweat, except that he did not place rocks in the flames. He started the fire with grass, dry leaves, little twigs and bits of wigwas as he had been taught long ago, the old teacher saying, "Nothing man-made, no paper, just natural things for connecting with creation; and no cigarette butts or gum wrappers." He had brought a folding lawn chair, placed the blanket in it, and nestled down. He watched the wind gusts bend the top of the big spruce tree on the riverbank and thought about his son's scaffold, switching and scraping back and forth. Then he retreated within himself, as he would have were he on a fast himself, and focussed his silent prayers on Joel's spiritual pilgrimage.

In the evening Uncle Viborg coasted to his parking spot and closed his car door quietly, lest sounds carried. It was the same protocol Carl had followed. The sound of a slammed car door, or even a mail box being opened and closed, carried far. Uncle was dressed oddly in pale pink, almost white slacks, cuffs tucked into white socks, a light-colored shirt and a washed-out baseball cap, its bill tilted up at a 45 degree angle. Carl was nonplussed, then amused until he realized that fussy, meticulous Viborg had thought of something he himself had overlooked. It was wood tick season and the first enthusiastic crop of parasites had emerged. Carl in his dark blue jeans and work shirt had been picking them off all day; Uncle, with his light-colored clothing, would have no such problem.

Viborg, tall and skinny, walked with head and shoulders thrust forward. His thick round glasses gave him an owlish look. Behind his back the youngsters called him Old Owl; to his face he was Shahshahwahbenais, falcon, and commanded respect. He had been encouraging them to speak the language, Thelberta growing up in a family that did not speak it, not wanting their children to be handicapped by being "too Indian" in a white society.

"Aneen wahsaygabow," he greeted Carl and rattled on in Indian knowing he was not being understood. He shook his head. "You really should learn the language. I'll go check the boy." He hesitated a moment as though to say something but said nothing about Carl keeping vigil and walked off.

Uncle took the roundabout trail that followed the truck tracks, then disappeared from view in the woods long before the hilltop. A buck trotted across the meadow heading for the woods, stopped as if watching, scenting the gaunt man in the light clothing, then veered off.

Carl could see nothing of what went on up on the hill. He assumed Uncle would have the boy climb down to relieve himself, would say prayers with him, answer any questions Joel had, and have him climb back up to his aerie.

Gone a long time. Was something wrong? Had the boy fallen? Was he ill? With every minute Carl considered other scenarios, each worse than the one before. Joel had a broken leg. He had a broken back. How would they carry him out? How close could the ambulance come? Where was the nearest telephone?

Uncle finally reappeared walking slowly in his almost dainty way, seemingly unconcerned but watching for gopher holes and, no doubt, wood ticks.

"He's doing fine," he said softly. "Didn't have his big dream yet, but he's in good shape."

"Up pretty high." Something midway between a question and a statement.

They looked at each other long moments, then Uncle said, "Nice fire. You'll be rebuilding the lodge this spring? Good. I'll be back tomorrow night to check on him. He's doing all right."

"Buck came out right after you went among the trees," Carl said.

"Yep. Saw it." Uncle again made as if to speak but changed his mind and left with a wave.

Carl dozed off and on. He woke once and it was dark. He put more wood on the fire. The wind woke him again later. Strong gusts from the southeast were bending the tops of the big trees around him, scudding last fall's leaves across the ground. Sparks flew from the fire. Lightning flashes beyond the horizon strobe-lighted the darkness. No moon, no stars. It would rain; it felt like it and the unruly wind seemed to say that it would happen.

Carl rose, found poles and rope, and put up a tarp to shelter the fire and himself, hoping Joel had a plastic sheet or some other waterproof cover. He knew the boy could not see him or the fire from his roost; perhaps he could sense that someone was out there giving him support.

When the rains came they were driven diagonally by blasts of wind that bent the trees. The tarp did not protect Carl very much and soon his clothes were damp, then wet, yet somehow the fire kept blazing away. The remainder of the night became a blur of fatigue and cold discomfort as episodes of violent rain and wind drove through and around. There were quiet spells, pauses in the water torture. He woke again as the sun rose in a passion-red sky: more storms to come. Red sky at night, sailors' delight; red sky in morning, sailors take warning.

The man fasted along with his son, willing himself out toward the boy in the tree, sitting in his chair wrapped in a blanket and an inadequate sheet of plastic, nurturing the fire. It did not rain any more all day and in the late afternoon Uncle returned.

"He's fine," the uncle said after having visited and prayed with Joel. "Didn't have his dream. Maybe tomorrow, fourth day. He's staying dry up there. You doing all right? Good."

That night the storm was more violent than before. Carl's lean-to collapsed but the fire did not go out. In first light he walked up the trail softly to where it turned sharply into the woods. He could make out the base of the trees holding the scaffold but not the scaffold itself nor its occupant. At least there was no sign of the scaffold or the boy on the ground. Carl put down tobacco and quietly returned to his post.

Time lost all dimension. He dozed, woke to keep fire, assessed the weather, and said prayers for his son. His wife visited twice but recognized Carl's trancelike state and left again as quietly as she had come. Uncle arrived, clad in pale lavender pants tucked into socks and light blue shirt. Again he stayed a long time and reported, "Joel is doing fine, just fine, nothing to worry about." The catclysmal dream had yet to come. "It's the fourth night. Maybe tonight." He had nothing else to say and left abruptly.

Off and on during the day the sun had broken through the cloud cover. Carl noticed the white cloth fluttering again, so perhaps Joel was drying out. But about nightfall clouds roiled and twisted and the storm broke with awful violence, once again bending the trees, whipping and shaking them. Once again Carl's flimsy shelter was blown apart but the fire continued to burn.

When rain and wind stopped, fireflies emerged into the cool stillness and then the other lights glittered in the sky. The storm had broken and the wild weather system moved on.

Daybreak. Another day. Sunny, steam rising from the saturated soil, then from his sodden clothing. Carl was subliminally aware of birds, ducks, geese, a fox crossing the meadow, does watering at river's edge. Aware of the sun's arc across the sky. Then Uncle standing beside him.

"He wants to stay another night," Uncle said. "Fifth night. I think I'll bring him in tomorrow evening whether he's had his vision or not. He'll have to bring the feather down, then we'll feast. Outside his little house. On the ground. Just family."

This was a sweet night, cool but not cold, and the air was pale honey. Carl rolled up in his blanket next to the fire.

"What will we do?" Thelberta wrung her hands as Carl entered the kitchen. "I'm on my time, and so's Melissa."

Carl stood stupefied, slow to register the words. He knew Thelberta and the girl wanted to be there, wanted to see Joel come walking out, wanted to hear about such of his experiences as he was allowed to relate, and feast him. They wanted to prepare the food, the chokecherry juice, boil the cedar medicine to bathe him. But it was not allowed. "I'll call my sisters," she said.

Joel came walking out slowly, steadily, carrying all his bedroll and gear, Uncle Viborg beside him. Carl saw them emerge from the hilltop woods and make their way step by slow step through the meadow. He fought the impulse to run to meet them, take his son's heavy load and carry it for him; it could not be. Joel had to walk home to his little cabin—only then could he put down his burden and climb to the roof to retrieve the eagle feather which had represented his continuing presence at the building while he had gone on the spirit journey up on the fasting scaffold in the tree.

As they drew near Carl saw his son's face, black with grime and exhaustion. He saw the look of triumph, of pride, the fleeting smile of love, and he wept as boy and Uncle passed in silence on the last steps of the exhausting pilgrimage. A boy had gone into the woods and a man returned. Tears of joy.

The two would need time at the cabin. Carl used it to retrieve the four sugar maple saplings he had dug up in the woods earlier and wrapped in wetted newspapers. He planted them in the four directions some distance from the altar and hung colored ribbons from the branches—colors for the Loon Clan, whom he thanked for guarding and helping his son, colors for Joel's name; maples to savor the sweetness of life and because the sap and sugar were the first fruits of the year, just as Joel's manhood had come to fruition; the four directions to center within creation, to honor its infinity. The vigil fire could now be allowed to burn itself out. Carl hauled water from the river to moisten the transplanted trees and force any remaining air from the roots.

He gently bathed Joel with cedar water, softly as he had so long ago when Joel had been an infant. Face, body, arms and hands, legs, feet, the soles on which one walked on the path of life, the young man half embarrassed, half grateful. The act of bathing was both comfort and symbolic of the rebirth, the new life consequent to the fast and the journey into the spirit world.

Uncle overseeing every detail and giving precise directions, Carl made the final preparations. The sisters had come bringing food. They sat in a circle around the blanket laden with food and drink.

As Uncle Viborg directed, Carl extended the first cup of water mixed with chokecherry juice to Joel to break his fast.

"This is for all the elderly and those alone and ill and in need." Joel rejected the cup, pointing to Uncle who drank it in their behalf.

He rejected the second cup. "This is for the women who give us all life, who carry new life in their bodies in water, who care for and protect the water." His Aunt Ruth drank it.

"This is for all the children, especially those who are abandoned or abused or poor and in need." His younger brother drank in their behalf.

The fourth cup he poured on the ground, honoring the earth.

Only then did he break his fast of six days and five nights with a sip of the liquid.

After the feast and the formalities when Uncle Viborg spoke praise of Joel, spoke about his not obtaining his vision dream ("there'll be other times, some important things happened to him out there"); and Joel spoke about some of what he had seen, heard, felt; and Carl spoke his respect and honor for his man-son, the joking and teasing began as they relaxed, sated. When the time came for Joel's vision dream he would not be able, allowed, to talk about it, and that was understood too. That would be private to him, between him and the spirits and his teacher. Now it was a time to celebrate.

"I've never seen anyone on a scaffold 35 feet up," Uncle said. "Couldn't believe it the first time I went out to check."

"Well, you said build a scaffold in a tree," Joel replied. "An eagle nest, you said. So all right, that's what I did."

Uncle Viborg shook his head. "Six feet, eight, maybe ten or twelve, I should have said."

"I felt you out there, Dad, giving me strength. Thanks, but I was safer in that world than in this one."

A few weeks later Carl's world collapsed, or so it seemed to him. One evening Uncle Viborg came to visit. The usually easy conversation somehow faltered and died and they sat in the living room in silence, increasingly uneasy, not knowing why. Finally Uncle dropped a bombshell, not wanting to do it. "Been talking to elders, now Joel's fasted. I'm sorry, Carl, but he can't be Mahng Dodaim like you and your kids have thought all this time. See, you're adopted. Dodaim doesn't come with adoption, whites can't have that, even if the ones adopted you gave a name, you can't get a clan. Only Indians. Kids with a white father are Migizi Dodaim, Eagle Clan."

For how long now—twenty, thirty years— Carl had thought himself Loon Clan, had prayed, had felt the clan strength in sore times, had treasured the portents, the feeling of protection. Gone?

The children shifted uncomfortably, glancing at their father, then looking away.

"I had to tell them," Uncle said. "They didn't want to believe it. I didn't either, but I knew it was so. I checked it out with the elders."

They waited for Carl to say something, to show a sign. Into the stunned silence he finally squeezed out, "Migizi is a noble dodaim. You kids can be proud." He did not want them to feel bad, to diminish their evolving sense of identity—that he knew on the instant. Inside himself it was another matter.

He was in shock. How often had he prayed to Mahng Dodaim? Worn gray and green? It was woven into the warp and woof of his spirituality, this more-than-symbol now taken away. Or had he ever had it? Fish out of water. Man without a country. Flotsam. No, flotsam had salvage value. Jetsam thrown overboard to lighten a load. And it was as though the children had been taken from him, they were not his any more. Would it be that way?

Would he still be able to function as ashkabewis, making fires for the sweats, taking care of the lodge? Make fires for the women's monthly moon ceremonies? Assist, be an integral part of the seasonal ceremonies held here and there drawing hundreds of people? Or gradually become a tolerated outsider?

"We love you," his children all said, but their voices came to him from far away. He was at the bottom of a deep well and the voices echoed from far, far above, scarcely audible. Could he still dance? Carry a pipe? Wear the embroidered vest on special occasions? Was he still the man he had felt himself to be? The same person? He had walked this way for so long, beginning even before he met and married Thelberta, that no other way existed for him any longer. Had it all been make-believe? An illusion? A fantasy?

And yet, and yet in his heart of hearts he also knew that hospitable, generous, openhearted and open-door Indians had time and again been taken over by their white guests. First it was one genuine, dedicated white allowed to sundance, to make devotions at the tree of life, to pierce and offer. Then another. Then less dedicated ones. Then groupies and tourists, even from abroad, and people with camcorders and tape machines until the sacred ceremony threatened to become a travesty, and the Lakota elders, after much thought and prayer and smoking many pipes reluctantly concluded that the sacred ceremonies had best be kept for the people of the blood, knowing that even some of them didn't practice the life to which they had dedicated themselves. Carl knew that, knew the white camel's nose under the tent too often meant no room left for the Indians. He knew also that increasingly over the years young people drifting to ceremonies, drawn in a search for their identities, were confused and then angered seeing whites participate: they are trying to take it away from us again, they thought and said. They are mocking us, making fun, yuppie wannabes. Carl had seen it happening and had not known what to do about it.

He knew too that there was a strong streak still, as in old times, that some of the ritual, some of the teachings, the medicines, the spells, had to be secret until earned, initiates told repeatedly: commit yourself, learn, acquire the accumulated lore and knowledge of millennia. Carl, witness to and helper at many ceremonies of the ancient religious society, had wanted to be initiated. The beauty, the deep sense of commitment to this way of life, were values he wanted from the inside out, not from the outside in. He had offered tobacco, asked to be admitted, to sit at the tree of life; the tobacco had been accepted but each year he was told: later, some other time, next year, until he realized he would never be initiated, and eventually he accepted this not as a rejection of him, but as an unfortunate but necessary integer of Indian survival. But now . . . what?

He put on a frozen-faced mask to Uncle, to his family, but when Viborg had left and the family fanned out Carl went outside to the woodshed and sat alone and in silence, still in shock. He was not sure what all this meant or portended, but he had a strong sense of calamity, of loss and dismay.

"Can I still carry my pipe?" Carl asked the old shaman, a friend and teacher over the years. Many people came to consult this man, learn from him, and each year he put acolytes and others out to fast. "Dance? Work for the lodge, the people?"

"I don't see why not," the shaman said, shaking his head, "I've known you a long time, I know where your heart is. Can't say I understand all this, there must be some kind of misunderstanding. I'll be visiting with the elders next month and ask. I'll get back to you. Now don't worry, it'll all work out."

Carl waited a long time but the shaman never got back to him. That of course was answer in itself. It went against the grain to gainsay anyone at any time.

He went to Viborg. "I don't know," Uncle shifted uncomfortably and would not look at him. "The old man asked me to see you, said the elders told him you could only feast with us, help on the outside. Not be inside, like at ceremonies."

"Not carry a pipe? Not work for the sweat lodge? Go into a sweat myself?" Carl's heart hammered, the blood pounded in his head until he felt the top would blow off.

Uncle Viborg shrugged. "Some say no, some yes," he waffled, not wanting to say something negative. But that was the meaning of it all right.

That's when the anger rose in Carl. He didn't say it aloud, just stood staring at Viborg, but he thought that if children of white fathers were Migizi Dodaim, then just about everyone was Migizi Dodaim because there were hardly any full-bloods left. That meant everyone was guilty of incest, forbidden marriage within your dodaim since time immemorial, unless they manufactured or created some other dodaim for themselves. He continued staring at Uncle Viborg, mouth clamped shut, his mind racing: reverse racism! Mixed-blood Indians overcompensating their traditionalism to prove something not needing proof! I've been partisan, my tribe right or wrong! I've guided, encouraged, even dragged my family to dances and ceremonies and now look . . . But he dropped it, did not say any of it. He knew it was anger of the moment covering up the hurt. The black hole inside consumed his heart.

Nothing changed in town, people still smiled at him. There were the little signs of recognition and acceptance as friends and acquaintances passed in stores or on the streets. There were no leper brands on his forehead, no letter A hanging around his neck, but his heart was sore and he felt lost.

Time came to take down the old sweat lodge and build a new one. Often in past years they had set a day, invited friends, brought food, and it was a special occasion full of fellowship and fun, but also in a way a sacred duty that went with being caretakers. Now it was as if a meteor had burst and could not be reconstituted.

"Are you going to put tobacco in the holes for the posts?" Joel asked. Carl had overlooked it.

Thelberta was full of advice and criticism about how Carl was laying the horizontal strips, something he had done countless times. She contradicted him when he gave instructions, telling the others to do things differently. The message was that he was not to be listened to, not to be minded, that he did not know what was to be done or how to do it.

Joel, Kit, and their two friends spoke in Indian, ignoring him. "What's a white guy doing telling us how to build a lodge?" one of the friends said and Carl understood. And Joel said, "He didn't give the sweat lodge teaching this time, the way you're supposed to, when there are newcomers." The friends had never put their hands on lodge-building before.

Kit chased Melissa, tackled her and rubbed dandelion chaff on her nose. Joel and his friends joined in the roughhouse and soon they were chasing each other, running through the incomplete lodge structure, shouting, screaming, leaping over the new altar.

"This is sacred work," Carl stopped them. "If you don't want to do it, go elsewhere to play."

It seemed he had lost his power and his moral suasion. That day they left the lodge unfinished to be completed on the morrow.

Before leaving Carl looked at the four maples, ribbons still aflutter, and grieved over the lost sweetness which now seemed beyond reach. The building of the lodge had always been like the start of a new year, a festival of sorts, a rededication. He felt this had been, somehow, a sacrilege. The spring renewal had been profaned and once again he felt he had been drummed out of the regiment, stepping out between the rank and file in dishonor to the accompaniment of the Rogue's March.

They stopped asking him to make fire for the full moon, did not tell him when there would be sweats or have him serve as ashkabewis. He was left out, isolated from the spiritual life that had been so much of the family cement. Then a day came when Thelberta said, "They sent word it's time for us to take down the lodge." He knew what she meant.

It was hard. The two of them working in silence took down the tarps and folded them. He cut the strings holding the horizontal branches to the vertical poles and pulled them out of the earth, his tears falling nonstop until every last thing had been removed, dragged into the woods, the altar levelled, and the white quartz Little Boy taken away and buried. Thelberta had left then, leaving behind a blanket torn in half, and he had lain on the ground pounding his fists into the earth, his face in the soil which swallowed his sobs, until for the first time in many, many years he spasmed into fetal rigidity and lost consciousness.

The sun had not quite set when his eyes opened. Soon the light would begin to diminish as the earth and he on it turned away from the sun, and then they would turn toward and into darkness. Carl tongued particles of earth out of his mouth. He sat up slowly, muscles and tendons weak in the lassitude following the seizure cramps.

He saw the altar and an eagle sitting on it.

Was he hallucinating? The crescent-moon-shaped altar which he and his wife had levelled was back . . . the Little Boy rock he had buried some distance away rose from its center . . . and there . . . there atop the rock sat Migizi, yellow talons curved around the white stone . . . blinking yellow eyes then . . . then . . . the second set of lids, the ones protecting its eyes when it dove, blinking from side to side like blue lightning. I'm imagining . . . this can't be . . . am I going mad? Don't return me to that black hole!

Was Migizi speaking to him? Saying, "Rituals are man's attempts to understand the great mystery. They are bridges humans build trying to span the infinite, seeking to cross the chasm of eternity. Man's rites are his striving for meaning and goodness in life. They are necessary means to a noble end. When they become ends in themselves sight is lost of the purpose. Man is a sojourner on this planet and in time, a pilgrim between the miracles of birth and death. Look! Look! Look up! When you hang your head you cannot see the stars of the Creator's Universe!"

Carl did look up then at the darkening sky and saw the evening star emerge, that bright harbinger of the nightly spectacle, illuminator of hope wherever one viewed the grand canopy. He felt awe at the beauty, the incomprehensible infinity, but glad to be part of it even if he could not understand it.

When his gaze turned back Migizi was gone. The altar had disappeared again, the Little Boy was nowhere to be seen.

"My imagination," Carl mumbled and rose.

He walked to where the altar had been, where he thought he had seen Migizi who had spoken to him.

There he found the large eagle feathers Migizi had left.